MARVEL
CAPTAIN MARVEL

A STUDIO PRESS BOOK

First published in the UK in 2020 by Studio Press,
an imprint of Bonnier Books UK,
The Plaza, 535 King's Road, London SW10 0SZ
Owned by Bonnier Books,
Sveavägen 56, Stockholm, Sweden

www.studiopressbooks.co.uk
www.bonnierbooks.co.uk

1 3 5 7 9 10 8 6 4 2

ISBN 978-1-78741-698-7

MIX
Paper from
responsible sources
FSC® C018072

Written by Sharon Gosling
Edited by Laura Pollard
Cover illustration by Derek Charm

A CIP catalogue for this book is available
from the British Library
Printed and bound in the UK

Sharon Gosling

AN ORIGIN STORY

CHAPTER 1
DISASTER IN THE ARCTIC

'Girl, are you *seeing* this?'

Over the phone, Spider-Woman's voice somehow managed to sound both horrified and just a tiny bit excited, which was actually pretty standard for Captain Marvel's friend.

Carol – Captain Marvel – stared at the video footage on her TV screen.

'Yeah,' she said. 'I'm seeing it.'

Something extremely bad was happening in the Arctic. The news programme was showing live footage of what looked like a volcano erupting from deep beneath a glacier. The ice was quaking with the force of a thousand bombs going off all at once, as something ripped its way up from far below the surface. Massive cracks began to appear in the ice, tearing jagged chunks out of the snow-covered landscape.

'There are people there,' said Spider-Woman. 'Look!'

The shaky footage was showing a ship caught amid the freezing waters, being thrown this way and that in the choppy ocean. As Captain Marvel watched, a huge cliff of ice sheared off from the quaking edge of the glacier and crashed into the water, sending an even larger wave towards the struggling ship.

'Have you got this?' asked Spider-Woman. 'I'm kind of tied up right now. You know I'd be there if I could, right? I'm not just leaving you to do this on your own because I hate the cold. I mean, I *do* hate the cold – snow, ugh, yadda yadda yadda – but that's beside the point.'

Carol grinned. 'Chill. Put your feet up. Have a snow cone.'

'Funny. You're just so *funny*, Carol, that's what I like about you.'

'Can't chat, stuff to do,' Captain Marvel told her friend, as she ran towards the open window of her apartment. 'I got this. Catch you later, Jess!'

She tossed her phone onto the couch and leapt up to her window ledge, pausing for a split second before throwing herself out the window.

The wind hit Carol in the face as she launched herself into the air, her heart beating a crazy rhythm in her chest. It didn't matter how many times she did this, flying just never grew old. How could it? She was flying! It was just the best feeling to be out here, to be free of gravity, to be free of everything, soaring away from the ground and into the sky.

Captain Marvel left New York City and North America behind, rising higher and higher until the edge of the continent curved away from her. She headed north, flying as fast as she could. She had to find a way to stop what was happening before the ice cap collapsed completely. But first, she had to save the people on that ship.

As she reached the ship, Captain Marvel could see that it was in real trouble. It was simply too small to navigate the huge waves crashing into it. Massive chunks of the glacier kept breaking off, plunging into the ocean and sending yet more water washing over the bucking ship. It made Carol think about what would happen if the whole ice cap melted – cities all over the world would suffer a similar fate.

She could see people on the ship's deck desperately clinging to whatever they could. It was going to sink if she couldn't save it, and quickly.

'You're the strongest woman in the world,' Captain Marvel reminded herself. 'You can do this.'

Carol shot towards the ship faster than a bullet from a gun. She hovered at the ship's prow, just above the icy water, feeling it splash against her suit as she found her grip.

Then she began to lift. The effort made her muscles burn, but the ship began to rise out of the waves, saltwater streaming from the hull. As another gigantic wave burst across her back, Captain Marvel gasped. Still, she didn't let go.

Second by second she gained momentum, shoving the ship clear of the waves until she could set it down on smoother waters again. She let it go and hovered above the deck, letting the water trickle off her suit.

The people on the deck of the ship started to notice her. They looked like the crew of a research vessel – these weren't seasoned deep-sea sailors. Were they scientists? Then Carol saw the logo on their jackets. It belonged to a global oil company.

She turned to look at the disaster still happening beneath the ice, then back at the people below her.

'Hey,' she said. 'Do you know what that is? Do you know what's happening out there?'

One of the men struggled to his feet, his face pale.

'We – we didn't know,' he stammered. 'We didn't know this would happen!'

Captain Marvel landed on deck, standing before him with her hands on her hips. 'You didn't know what would happen? What did you do?'

'We found something beneath the ice,' the man said. 'It must have been there for centuries, but with climate change, the ice has now melted enough for us to detect it.'

'What is it?' Carol demanded. 'What did you find?'

'We don't know. Some sort of machine. We thought – *I* thought – that if we could get it out, we might be able to use it to mine the oil that's below the surface. But something activated it before we could get it out.'

'Now it's destroying the entire ice cap,'

said a women next to him. 'If that happens, these waves are going to look like droplets in comparison with what will come next. It will destroy *everything*. Earth will never be the same.'

'Not if I can stop it,' said the super hero. 'Get out of here. Get the ship as far away as you can. I'll deal with this – whatever it is.'

Captain Marvel flew into the air again, speeding back towards the rupturing mass of land and ice. A shape was visible now, a dark shadow was forcing its way towards the surface from beneath the splintering ice and snow.

Something punched its way free of the ice. It was a massive metal hand. It smashed down into the snow, clutching for grip as it hauled itself free of its icy prison.

'It's a robot,' Captain Marvel said aloud. 'It's a giant metal robot! Why is it *always* robots?'

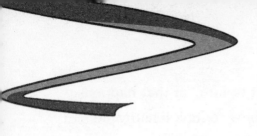

CHAPTER 2
A MIDNIGHT ADVENTURE

Sometime after midnight on a cold, clear night, the silver-and-red toy robot that Carol had just got for her fifth birthday decided to wake her up and start talking.

'*Robot Supreme to Carol Squirt Danvers,*' it said, in a low voice that sounded a lot like her big brother Stevie. '*Directive from Robot Control says: Wake up! You're missing all the fun!*'

Carol blinked her bleary eyes and stared at the robot. It had snuck under the duvet she had pulled up over her head.

'What?' she asked.

'*Not "what?",*' the robot corrected her

primly. *'Sorry!'*

Carol blinked again. 'Sorry, what?'

'Never mind,' said Stevie in a hushed voice, appearing from the side of the bed and dropping the robot on her pillow. 'Just wake up!'

Carol Danvers' childhood home was in a quiet suburb of Boston, where she lived with her mum Marie, her dad Joe and her two stepbrothers, Stevie and Joe Junior. Though her brothers were a few years older than her, they never minded their little sister hanging around with them. Like now, for instance, when Stevie had snuck into her room to wake her up to play, when she really should have been fast asleep.

'What's happening?' Carol mumbled, still sleepy.

'Ssh,' Stevie whispered. 'Come on, Squirt, we're going on an adventure.'

To five-year-old Carol, the idea of an adventure in the middle of the night was both exciting and scary. She sat up and rubbed her eyes. 'An adventure? Where? Are

Mom and Dad coming?'

'Nope, it's just us and Joe. You'd better hurry, or you'll miss it. Put on the warmest sweater and socks you've got.'

'Are we going very far?' Carol asked.

'Yes,' Stevie said. 'We're going into space. Hurry up!'

Carol rushed to do as her brother said and then followed him out of her room and down the hallway, treading on tiptoe past their parents' bedroom.

She held her breath as they crept down the stairs, avoiding the one that always creaked. Once they were downstairs, she looked around for her other brother.

'Where's Joe?'

'He's already started the adventure,' Stevie told her. 'We're late!'

Stevie took Carol's coat from the hook in the hallway and made her put it on, as he quietly opened the door. Then they went out into the garden. At first Carol couldn't see anything because it was so dark.

'Can't we use a flashlight?' she asked.

'No!' Stevie told her. 'There need to be as few lights as possible or your eyes won't adjust. Come on.'

He led Carol further into the garden.

'Hey, Squirt,' said a voice near Carol's left foot. 'You made it, then.'

It was her brother Joe. He was lying on his back on the grass, zipped inside a sleeping bag. There were two other sleeping bags laid out beside him.

'Quick, get in,' Stevie told her, as he sat down and began to get into his own bag.

Carol did as she was told. 'I thought you said we were going into space?' she asked, disappointed that they hadn't gone any further than their own backyard. She'd imagined a beautiful silver rocket carrying them up into the night sky.

'We are,' Stevie told her. 'Lie back and look at the stars.'

She did. Carol had never really paid attention to the stars properly before. The more she stared into the darkness, the more pinpricks of light she could see. They were never-ending, and there was so much to take in that her eyes could barely manage it.

Joe's watch started beeping, a tiny sound muffled by all his layers of clothing.

'Okay,' her brother said, as he turned off the alarm. 'Showtime, people.'

'Watch really, really carefully,' Stevie whispered to Carol. 'You'll see something moving. It's going to come over the top of the house.'

All three of them were silent, but Carol didn't know what she was looking for.

'There!' said Joe. 'There it is!'

'I can't see it,' Carol cried. 'What does it look like?'

'Ssh,' Stevie said. 'Look again. It's a light, and it'll be moving.'

'A shooting star?'

'No, slower than that. Look carefully.'

Carol squinted. Then she saw it! A bright light, just like a star, but it was moving

16

through the night sky in an arc, right over
their house.

'What is it?' she asked in wonder.

'It's the International Space Station,'
Joe told her. 'You can't always see it from
Boston, but tonight you can, just for as long
as it takes to travel through our sky.'

Stevie nudged her. 'There are six astronauts
up there right now, Squirt,' he said.

Carol watched the little light that was the
ISS sail steadily over their heads. She tried
to imagine what it would be like to be one of
the astronauts inside. How would it feel to be
out there, among all those stars, in space?

They watched the light move until it
disappeared from view. Then they watched
the stars a little longer.

'Right,' Stevie said after a while. 'We'd
better get you back to bed, or we'll all be in
trouble in the morning.'

Carol didn't move. She was too busy
studying the stars.

Stevie nudged her again. 'Squirt?' he asked,

as Joe unzipped his sleeping bag and stood up. 'You fallen asleep?'

'No,' Carol told him, still looking up at the stars. 'Just thinking.'

'Oh? About what?'

'I'm going to go up there one day. I'm going to go to space.'

Her brothers both laughed, though Carol didn't think they were being mean.

'Good for you,' said Joe. 'Our little sister, the astronaut.'

* * *

The next day, Carol asked her mum to take her to the local library.

'I want to learn about space,' she said, over breakfast.

Her dad stopped eating his oatmeal. Her mum and dad shared a look that Carol didn't understand.

'Please, Mommy. If I'm going to be an astronaut, I need to know all about the stars.'

'You don't want to be an astronaut, honey,' said her dad. 'It's dangerous.'

'I do,' Carol said, stoutly.

'You could be an engineer instead,' her mum pointed out. 'You could build space shuttles. That would be cool, wouldn't it?'

'I want to be an astronaut,' Carol insisted.

'It can't hurt to look at some books, can it?' Carol's mum said to her dad.

He sighed. 'Well, if you think it's a good idea...'

They went to the local library and asked the librarian for books about space. The librarian seemed pleased to be asked and pulled out several volumes for Carol to borrow.

'Is this for a school project?' The woman asked.

Carol shook her head. 'No. I'm going to be an astronaut.'

The librarian grinned. 'That's a wonderful goal to have. Did you know that before you can be an astronaut, you need to know how to fly an aircraft? That's why one of the main routes into the astronaut programme is to join the air force.'

'Oh,' said Carol. 'Then I guess I need to learn to fly.'

The librarian smiled and pulled a thick tome from a higher shelf.

'This is meant for adults really, but I think it'll be perfect for you. It's about one of my heroes. Her name is Helen Cobb. She's a pilot and she's broken all sorts of records. This is a book about her by a journalist called Tracey Burke. She followed Cobb around for a year, writing about her. I think you'll love it. It's got a lot of great photographs, too.'

Carol took the book – it was big and heavy – and looked at the cover. It showed a photograph of a smiling woman standing in front of a beautiful silver plane.

The plane reminded Carol of the rocket she'd imagined bursting out of their backyard.

She didn't hear anything else the librarian or her mum said that afternoon – she was too busy looking at photographs of her new hero.

CHAPTER 3
HIGHER, FURTHER, FASTER

Carol Danvers liked school. She particularly liked anything to do with science. Whenever she had to do a presentation to her classmates, it would be about space or flying.

Helen Cobb was Carol's absolute hero, and when it was her turn to choose what to play at break time, she would take her friends on amazing expeditions in her imaginary aircraft. They would burst through Earth's atmosphere and cross space itself, discovering new planets and exploring new landscapes. She ran everywhere as fast as she could, feeling the wind blast across her cheeks and imagining what it would be like to travel faster than anyone else had ever gone before, to fly even faster than Helen Cobb.

Carol hadn't forgotten that to be a real astronaut she needed to learn to fly. She had never been in a plane before, though. One day when she was out shopping with her family, Carol saw a colourful poster for a tourist flight in a small aeroplane. The advertisement offered a half-an-hour flight over the bay in a Cessna 172, a tiny aircraft that had only four seats. It was white, not silver, but to Carol it looked like something straight out of one of her dreams.

'Mom, Dad!' she said, excited. She pulled her mum by the sleeve and pointed at the poster. 'Look! Can we go?'

Her dad read the poster with a frown. 'Of course we can't, don't be ridiculous.'

'Oh, please!' Carol begged. 'It's my birthday soon.'

'No,' said her dad. 'And that's final.'

Carol looked at her mum, pleading with her eyes. 'Mom, this is the only thing I want for my birthday. Please?'

Her mum looked at her dad. 'It couldn't do any harm, Joe. If it's really what she wants.'

'Marie, look at it,' he replied impatiently. 'It's only got four seats. It looks like a tin can. It'd be like flying in a deathtrap. No.'

Her mum sighed as her dad stalked away, then she smiled down at Carol before catching up with him. As Carol gazed at the poster she heard them talking.

'Why are you encouraging her?' her dad asked.

'It's just a pleasure flight, Joe, that's all. And she wants it so much.'

'It's too dangerous, and you know it.'

Carol wanted to ask why it was dangerous for her to fly when so many other people did it every day, but she didn't. She ended up getting a new bike for her eighth birthday instead. She smiled when she saw it wrapped up with a big red ribbon and bow, even though it hadn't been exactly what she wanted.

'Wow, Squirt,' said Stevie. 'Looks like you'll be giving Joe and me a run for our money on the ramps, eh?'

Carol grinned. The ramps! She'd been so caught up with wanting to go in the aeroplane that she'd forgotten all about them. On an abandoned lot at the end of their road, Stevie, Joe and a load of their friends had built a series of obstacles to jump over. She couldn't borrow either of her brothers' bikes because they were too big for her. Now she could join in.

For the next few weeks, Carol spent as much time as she could on the obstacle course. Whenever she wasn't at school, that's where she and her friends would be. Some of the ramps were scary at first, and even Stevie was worried about her jumping over them.

'You don't have anything to prove, Squirt,' he said. 'Having a bike is supposed to be fun. Don't do it if you're afraid.'

'I'm not afraid,' Carol said. 'I can't be afraid.'

'What do you mean?' her brother asked.

'I'm going to be an astronaut,' Carol reminded him. 'I'm going to go into space. I can't be afraid of going higher or faster. That's what people who go into space do, isn't it? They don't stop because they're scared.'

Stevie shook his head with a smile and ruffled her hair. 'You, kid sister, are one of a kind.'

Still, Carol *was* scared when she rode over the big ramp for the first time. It looked as if she was going to launch herself straight into the air. She sat on her bike, one foot on the ground and the other on her pedal as she bit her lip and tried to prepare.

She looked up at the blue sky overhead and thought about Helen Cobb. How was Carol going to break any records if she was afraid to ride her bike? She had to do this. She had to.

Carol pushed off and pedalled hard down the short hill that led to the jump. When she got to the ramp, she stopped pedalling and just gripped the handlebars. At the last minute she almost stopped herself by slamming down her feet, but she thought about those astronauts up there in the International Space Station, gritted her teeth and hunkered down.

The bike flew off the end of the ramp and the air hit her in the face and, just for an instant, just for a few seconds, Carol felt what it would be like to fly. She laughed and wanted it to go on forever, wanted to soar straight up into the sky and carry on flying, but the laws of gravity and her bike had other ideas.

Carol saw the ground coming up at her too quickly. She tried to brace herself for the impact, tried to land the way her brother Joe had told her to, but it was no good. The bike's front wheel jinked left and Carol flew to the right, crashing to the ground with a *thump!*

She felt a sharp, horrible pain in her wrist and screamed. The pain went on and on, but after a while, Carol didn't care. Not even when her dad got angry at her for doing something so dangerous. Not even when she ended up having to wear a cast for six weeks.

She didn't care because she knew what flying was like now. It was the best feeling in the world, just like she'd always known it would be.

CHAPTER 4
SUMMER SURPRISE

Every summer, Carol and her family went on holiday to Harpswell Sound in Maine. They had a little house near the water, where Uncle Richie – her dad's brother – kept a fishing boat. Carol had been going there since she was a baby, and she always loved it. The whole family would be together for the summer, and the days seemed endless, filled with sunshine, blue skies and fun.

The year that Carol turned ten, the Danvers family were in Harpswell Sound as usual. Their friend Louis was there too – his family also had a holiday home in the same area, and Carol and Louis always met up over the summer.

'So, have you seen the poster?' Louis asked Carol, as they sat on the Danvers' porch on the first day of the vacation.

'What poster?' Carol asked.

Louis stood up. 'Come on. Let's go into town and I'll show you. I haven't had a Brain Freezer yet!'

Brain Freezers were a tradition for them. Carol and Louis would compete with each other to see who could eat the biggest chunk of the frozen ice pop without getting a brain freeze. Carol always won, mainly because she never let on that she had a headache from the ice pop, even when she did.

Carol went into the house and shouted for her mum. 'Mom! Can I have some money to get a Brain Freezer with Louis?'

'Take ten dollars out of my purse,' Marie called back.

They got on their bikes and cycled all the way to the store, laughing and joking, glad that it was summer. After they'd chosen their favourite flavours, Louis led Carol over the road and pointed to a poster that had been pasted on the wall opposite.

'See?' he said, his mouth full of ice pop.

Carol stared at the poster – her own lolly forgotten. The poster was for The Great State of Maine Air Show, which was being held at the airport at Brunswick, only thirty minutes' drive away. What really caught Carol's eye, though, was the picture of a smiling woman standing in front of a gleaming silver plane.

SPECIAL GUEST! proclaimed a banner across the middle of the poster. *RECORD-BREAKING PILOT HELEN COBB IN HER FAMOUS T-6 AEROPLANE!*

'It's her, isn't it?' Louis asked. 'The pilot you're always talking about?'

Carol dropped her Brain Freezer and cycled all the way back to the summer house. When she got there, she yelled for her mum and dad. Her dad came running, a worried look on his face.

'What is it?' he shouted, grabbing her shoulders. 'What's happened?'

'It's Helen Cobb!' Carol cried. 'She's going to be here! In Maine! She's going to be at the air show next weekend! Can we go? Can we?'

Carol's dad let her go and stepped back, his expression turning angry. 'Is that all? I thought something bad had happened!'

'Please say we can go, Dad!' Carol begged. 'Please! I'm never going to get this chance again. She's going to be in her T-6!'

Carol's dad turned to Marie. 'This is your fault,' he told her. 'I said we shouldn't encourage her.' He stalked away, leaving Carol confused.

'What did I do?' Carol asked, trying not to cry. 'I just want to go to the air show, that's all. I just want to see Helen Cobb.'

Her mum hugged her and stroked her hair. 'I know, honey. You didn't do anything wrong. Your dad just worries about you, that's all.'

Carol sniffed, bunching her hands into fists. 'Why me? Why doesn't he worry about

Stevie and Joe? Stevie says he wants to join the army, and Dad doesn't care about that!'

'It's not that he doesn't care,' her mum told her. 'Of course he cares. He just worries about you more, that's all.'

'But *why?*'

Her mum shook her head. 'It's difficult to explain, Carol. Look, you go out and play with Louis and the boys. I'll see what I can do about us all going to the air show.'

Whatever her mum said, it worked, because on Saturday morning, all five of the Danvers were on their way to Brunswick. Carol was so excited she could barely breathe. She pressed her nose up against the car window as they drove into the busy airport car park.

Hundreds of people were attending and aeroplanes were already taking off. An announcer was explaining what the spectators were seeing, over a loudspeaker.

Cobb wouldn't be flying for a while, so the family wandered around, looking at the exhibits. Through the crowds, Carol spotted a recruitment stall for the US Air Force.

'Can we go and look?' Carol asked her mum. 'I can ask them about space programmes.'

'You're too young,' her dad said. 'Come on, let's get a hot dog before we watch your pilot.'

Carol reluctantly let herself be led away.

But she had insisted that they leave home early, so they got a good spot for watching Helen Cobb and her plane. When the pilot taxied out onto the runway, Cobb kept her cockpit open and waved to the spectators. Carol stood and cheered, waving back.

Then the pilot slid the cockpit shut and the silver T-6 picked up speed, lifting off and into the air with a roar of its single engine. The aeroplane flew higher and higher into a massive backwards arc overhead.

Carol watched, mesmerised, as Cobb traced figures of eight in the sky and looped-the-loop, the silver of her aircraft catching the sun and gleaming like a miniature star.

When the performance was over, Cobb brought the T-6 down to land smoothly on the runway and opened her cockpit again to wave at the crowds. Carol tried to imagine what it must feel like, to know that you could take off at any moment and soar into the air.

Later, Carol used the cover of the crowds to slip away from her family and make her way to the pilot's backstage area.

'Hey,' said one of the men guarding the entrance. 'You can't come in here unless you've got a backstage pass.'

'But I just want to meet Helen Cobb,' Carol said. 'I'm going to be a pilot just like her one day. I just want to ask her—'

The guard crossed his arms, his eyes hidden behind dark sunglasses. 'Sorry, kid. Like I said.'

'But—'

'Where are your parents?' he interrupted. 'What's your name?'

'I'm Carol Danvers. I just want to—'

The guard nodded at his partner, who went over to a tannoy system. A second later Carol heard her name being announced over the loudspeaker.

'Would the parents of Carol Danvers please come to the backstage gate immediately.'

Carol's heart sank.

Her dad was so mad that she had wandered off alone that he decided they would leave immediately.

'I can't trust you, can I?' he said angrily, as he marched Carol back to the car. 'I knew coming here was a mistake. We've got to get all this nonsense about flying out of your head.'

'It's not nonsense,' Carol shouted, yanking her hand out of his and stopping dead. 'I'm going to be a pilot, Dad. I'm going to go to space. Why don't you want me to do that? Why can't you just be on my side?'

'I'm your father,' he said. 'It's my job to keep you safe. That's the side I'm on!'

'But—'

Carol's mum put her hand on her daughter's shoulder. 'That's enough for now,' she said. 'Let's just go home.'

Carol got into the car and sat fuming in the back. She didn't speak to her dad for the rest of the journey. Halfway home, Stevie nudged her and then glanced at their father to make sure he wasn't looking. He carefully pushed something towards Carol, and then winked at her.

It was a brochure all about how to get into the United States Air Force. Stevie must have heard what she'd said to their dad!

Carol snuck a look inside. There was a lot that she didn't understand, but she didn't care. It seemed as if Stevie was on her side, even if her dad wasn't.

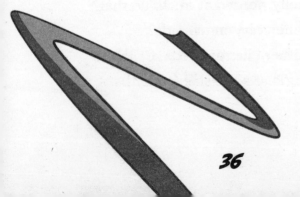

CHAPTER 5
CAPTAIN SHOOTING STAR

'I'm sorry,' Carol's dad said over breakfast the next morning. 'I'm sorry for getting angry. I just worry about you, that's all.'

'I know, Dad,' Carol replied, staring at her bowl of cereal – even though she didn't know, not really. She didn't understand. She'd said as much to her mum the night before, but Marie Danvers had told Carol that all she really needed to know was that her dad loved her very much.

'But what if he never understands that I really am going to be an astronaut?' Carol had asked.

'I know that's what you want now,' her mum said. 'But that might change, Carol. You don't know.'

'I do know,' Carol insisted. 'I don't care how hard it is or how much Dad is against it. It's what I'm going to do.'

Her mum had just hugged her, hard, and sighed.

Now Carol was sitting at the breakfast table pretending she didn't mind that her dad didn't want her to follow her dreams.

'Look,' he said. 'I'm going to make it up to you. Uncle Richie's lent me his fishing boat for the day so that I can take you out in it.'

Carol brightened up at that. She loved being out on the boat. With the wind in her face, if they were going fast enough, she could pretend she was flying.

'Thanks, Dad!'

'Why don't you see if Louis wants to come? Tell him to bring his fishing rod if he does.'

Marie came too, but Stevie and Joe had plans with some other summer friends and decided to stay behind.

'We'll see you later, Squirt,' said Joe. 'Don't fall overboard, all right?'

It was a bright, sunny day, and Carol was happy and excited as her dad piloted the boat out of the harbour. The seabirds were wheeling around the cliffs, screeching their high-pitched calls as they dipped and swooped. The ocean was calm, with only a slight wind. The boat picked up pace as they cleared the bay and headed out onto the sound, cutting smoothly through the waves.

'Well,' Carol's dad shouted to her over the boat's motor. 'I think today it might be time that you take the helm. What do you say?'

Carol couldn't believe it. She'd never been allowed to take the wheel before. 'Really?'

'Sure,' said her dad, waving her over. 'Come over here and I'll show you what to do.'

Within minutes, Carol was in control of Uncle Richie's boat. It was an amazing feeling. 'Can I go faster?' she asked her dad.

He smiled. 'All right. Just a little.' He touched a handle to her right. 'Push that forward. Carefully – take it steady.'

Carol let out a whoop as the boat zoomed over the waves, faster and faster. Louis laughed at her excitement, even though he was just as excited himself.

'We'll have to give you a new name,' he said, shouting over the noise of the wind and the boat. 'How about... Captain Shooting Star?'

Carol laughed. 'I like it!'

They stayed out on the boat for hours. For lunch, Carol's dad barbecued the fish they caught, right there on the deck. Afterwards, Carol and Louis lay on their stomachs on the prow, looking out at the water.

When they got back into harbour, they found Stevie and Joe waiting for them, both pink from having caught the sun.

'We're off to get doughnuts,' said Stevie, to Carol and Louis. 'Want to come?'

'Yes!' They both shouted, together.

'All right,' said Carol's dad. 'But be sensible. All of you. All right?'

The four of them bought doughnuts, but Stevie surprised Carol by buying a kite as well.

'We can fly it from the dock,' he pointed out. 'Not quite like having your own plane, I know, but until you do...'

'Ah, forget that,' Joe said. 'Let's see who can jump the furthest off the jetty.'

'Dad told us to be sensible,' Carol pointed out. 'That doesn't sound very sensible to me.'

Joe sensed an opportunity to tease his sister. 'Oh? Sounds like you're... scared.'

Carol puffed out her chest. 'I'm not scared!'

Joe began strutting around making chicken noises as the others laughed. '*Pwak-pwak-pwak!* My little sister's a chicken!'

'I am NOT!'

To prove it, Carol took a flying leap off the end of the jetty, without even stopping to take off her shoes. She heard the boys shouting as she splashed into the cool water. Then she kicked hard, swimming back to the surface to find them all struggling out of their shoes, eager to prove they could jump even further.

They stayed there all afternoon. Carol always jumped the furthest.

'I think it's because you're completely fearless, Squirt,' Stevie said. 'You're just not afraid of anything.'

'I'm afraid of plenty of things,' she told him, taking a huge bite out of a doughnut, liking the way the sugar stuck to her lips. 'I just don't let that stop me trying, that's all.'

By the time they'd eaten all the doughnuts they were excited from the rush of sugar. Stevie suggested they fly the kite, so they raced each other up the path to the cliff, unfurling it right at the top and watching it fly in the wind, dipping and swooping as wildly as a seabird.

CHAPTER 6
METEOR SHOWER

Two nights later, after Carol had gone to bed, she was looking at her USAF Academy brochure with her pocket flashlight under the covers. She had done this every night since Stevie had picked up the brochure, learning about the air force's requirements for new recruits. There was a lot she would have to learn if she wanted to get a place when she was older.

There was a sound at her window. Carol switched off her torch and stuck her head out from beneath the covers. After a moment, it came again – three little taps, then a pause, then another tap. She grinned to herself and climbed out of bed, creeping across the floor without a sound.

Joe was crouching outside on the roof. Carol unlatched the window and he helped her lift it.

'Come on,' he whispered. 'We've got blankets.'

Carol followed him and together they made their way to where Stevie was already sitting. The three of them did this every now and then. Between Carol's window and the window of the room her two brothers shared there was a flat ledge, perfect for stargazing.

'What are we looking for?' Carol asked, settling herself between the boys.

'Nothing in particular,' Stevie told her. 'Just felt like getting out of the house for a while, that's all.'

Carol said nothing to that. Stevie and their dad had been arguing lately. She looked up at the stars. Here in Harpswell Sound there was far less light pollution than back home, and

the night sky was so clear that she could see
the wide, ghostly smudge of the Milky Way
right above them.

'Look,' Joe said, pointing into the distance.
'No, too late, you've missed it – it was a
shooting star.'

'There's another,' Stevie said a moment
later. 'And another!'

Carol began to see them too – not just a
single shooting star, but several bright lights
streaking across the sky, one after the other.

'It's a meteor shower!' she said, amazed.

'Whoa,' said Stevie. 'I've never seen
anything like this before.'

The more they looked, the more they saw.
It seemed as if the entire night sky was full
of meteors, all skimming off the surface of
Earth's atmosphere. Then Carol's attention
was taken by one that seemed to be coming
lower and lower. She pointed it out.

'That's a meteorite,' she said. 'That's what
it's called when a piece of space rock makes
it through the atmosphere. It hasn't burned

up. It's going to make landfall!'

Joe nudged her. 'Geek.'

Carol wrapped her arms around her knees
and rested her chin on them, keeping her
eyes fixed on the burning ball of rock that
had come from outer space. 'I've got to know
all this stuff,' she said, 'if I want to be an
astronaut.'

The lump of space rock shot across their
field of vision before disappearing into the
darkness. Somewhere a long way away, a
car alarm started up, wailing into the night.
Carol stood up.

'We should go and find it,' she said. 'It
might have come down in town!'

Stevie grabbed Carol's arm and pulled her
down again. 'You must be joking,' he said.
'Dad would have our guts if we snuck out
now. Besides, we'll never find it. It could be
anywhere.'

'But—'

'Forget it, Squirt,' Stevie said, in a tone of
voice that wasn't to be argued with. 'You can

look for it tomorrow.'

Carol gave up and carried on watching the stars instead. The meteor shower had finished, but it was still an amazing sight.

'You really want to go up there one day?' Joe asked her. 'Out there, into all that nothing?'

'It's not nothing,' Carol said. 'It's space, and it's full of things we haven't seen yet. And yes, I'm going. Whatever it takes.'

Stevie put an arm around her shoulders and squeezed lightly. 'I believe you can do whatever you want to, kid sis,' he said. 'And I'll be with you one hundred per cent – as long as you're not just doing it to run away.'

'The way you are by joining the army, you mean?' Carol asked, and Joe snorted a laugh.

'Come on,' Stevie said, getting up. 'It's time for bed, smarty-pants.'

* * *

The next day, Carol gulped down her breakfast and ran out of the house before anyone other than her mum was up. She cycled over to Louis's place, dropped her bike on the lawn and threw stones at his bedroom window until she saw his face looking out.

'Captain Shooting Star!' he said blearily. 'What do you want?'

'Come on,' Carol said. 'We've got a meteorite to find!'

'A what?'

'A meteorite! An actual rock from outer space! I think it landed somewhere near town. Come and help me find it!'

Louis sighed. 'Can I have breakfast first? It's not even seven o'clock!'

They searched every street of the little town for hours, and when they couldn't find any sign of the fallen space rock there, they moved on to the surrounding woods. They asked everyone they passed if they'd seen anything out of the ordinary, but the answer was always no.

'Come on,' Louis said, eventually. 'Mom gave me enough money for Brain Freezers.

Let's go and get some.'

As they were riding along the main road into town, they saw a group of older boys gathered around something in a back alley. Carol slowed to a stop and watched. Louis realised she wasn't with him and circled back around.

'What is it?' he asked.

Carol nodded at the group of kids, who seemed to be laughing at something. 'What are they doing?'

Louis looked and shrugged, a worried look on his face. 'I don't know, and I don't care. Neither should you. Come on.'

'They're teasing something,' Carol said. 'What if it's a kid?'

'We can't go up against all of them,' Louis said nervously. 'Just leave it.'

Carol turned and looked at him, hard. 'Is that what you'd want me to do if they'd got *you* in a corner?'

Louis threw his arms up. 'Just because I called you Captain Shooting Star doesn't

make you a super hero! They'll eat you alive!
We can go and find someone to help, but—'

'Too late,' she told him, because a couple
of the boys had seen them and were nudging
each other. She looked at Louis. 'You can go
if you want. But I'm going to help.'

'Going to help who?' Louis hissed, as Carol
lifted her chin and rode into the alleyway. 'You
don't even know – oh, for crying out loud!'

'What do you want, little girl?' one of the
boys asked. 'Looking for your mommy?'

'Whatever you're doing, stop it,' Carol
said, in a loud, clear voice.

More of the boys turned to look at her.
Some of them had sticks. The one who'd
asked the question began to smirk. 'Or what?
What are you going to do, little girl? Are you
going to scream?'

Carol was scared, but the way he kept
saying the word 'girl', made her angry. She
climbed off her bike.

'No,' she said, as the boys began to
advance towards her. 'I don't scream.'

There was a bit of laughter. The whole pack of kids were coming towards her now.

'You sure about that?' one of them asked, still sniggering.

'Yes,' Carol said. 'I'm sure.'

Then she bellowed. It wasn't a scream – this came from her belly, and it was more like a roar. Carol Danvers was angry, bunching her hands into fists and standing her ground. A few of the bigger boys looked startled – it wasn't what they were expecting. Carol's yell echoed off the red brick walls and carried out into the street.

'Hey,' came an adult voice, from behind them. 'What's going on down there? What are you boys doing?'

That was enough to make them all run. Every boy fled down the alley and away, taking a wide berth around the little girl who had yelled at them.

Carol stood still for a second as the boys' running footsteps echoed away.

'Wow,' said Louis, into the silence that

followed. 'Maybe you really are a super hero! What made you do that?'

Carol turned to look at him with a faint smile. 'It was my dad,' she said. 'He told me once. "Kid," he said, "they'll expect you to scream, but they won't expect you to bellow. It'll surprise them, give you enough time to run away."'

'Except that you didn't run away,' Louis pointed out.

Carol looked back towards the end of the alleyway. 'If I'd done that then we wouldn't have been able to help whatever they were tormenting, would we?'

Louis shrugged. 'I can't see anything, can you? Maybe whoever it was got away while you were yelling.'

'Maybe...'

Then they heard it. A very small mew, coming from a pile of abandoned boxes in one damp corner. It was a tiny, terrified kitten.

Louis scooped it up and put it inside his hoodie.

CHAPTER 7
PLANS FOR
THE FUTURE

Carol's determination to become an
astronaut didn't change as the years went
on. When she was eleven, she snuck into a
career fair meant for much older students.
One of the stalls there caught her eye –
it was for an engineering lab that was
pioneering technology for private space
programmes.

Carol went over to look at the information.
The woman behind the counter smiled at
her.

'If you don't mind me saying so, you look a
little young to be here,' she said.

Carol nodded. 'I am. But I want to be an astronaut, and I know that to get there will take
a lot of dedication. I figure starting early is a good idea.'

The woman laughed. 'Well, that's admirable. Let me show you the type of work our company is doing, and we can talk about what path you might want to follow. I'm Penny.'

'I'm Carol.'

Penny spent some time explaining the sort of science degrees that would help Carol find a job with her company, and the type of roles she could do there. It gave Carol a lot to think about. She already enjoyed science and worked hard in those subjects, but she would need to focus on them even more from now on.

Carol stuffed some of the company's leaflets into her school bag. As she was leaving, she saw the stall for the US Air Force, and went to talk to them, too. They listened carefully to what Carol had to say about wanting to be an astronaut and were just as patient in explaining what she would need to do in order to pass the entrance exams and get into the academy's flight-training programme.

'It's not just about study,' the USAF officer explained. 'You also need to meet the fitness level requirements. I can give you some information that tells you exactly what you'll need to do.'

Carol went home that night with a lot to read and even more to think about. The next day over breakfast, she told her mum she wanted to enrol in her school's athletics club.

'Really?' her mum said, surprised. 'What's brought this on?'

'I just think it would be a good idea to raise my fitness level,' Carol said, as she ate her oatmeal. 'Can I?'

Marie Danvers smiled. 'I think it's a great idea.'

Soon Carol was running every day. It felt

natural to her, and even though it was hard work, she loved it. Her coaches encouraged her and for a while Carol even wondered whether she should concentrate on becoming an Olympic champion, she enjoyed running so much! But every time she looked up at the stars on a clear night, Carol felt a pull towards them, as if every fibre of her being was telling her she belonged up there, in space.

She spent her every spare minute reading books about science and the theory of future technologies.

'You've got to lighten up, Squirt,' Stevie said, when he came home from his army training for a visit. 'Have some fun, why don't you? Make some friends.'

'I've got friends!' Carol retorted. 'We run together. But this is important, Steve. I want to do this. I want to get into a good college.'

Her dad overheard this conversation. 'College!' he said. 'And who's going to pay for that? Won't be me, not if you're still talking about being an astronaut.'

'Dad,' Stevie said. 'Can't you tell that it's not just a pipe dream any more? I think Carol's got a real chance. She's smarter than the rest of us, and it's clear she's got the determination.'

'That's enough,' said their father. 'We can't afford to pay the fees those sorts of places want, and that's final.' He left the room.

'Why is he so against me doing this?' Carol asked Stevie, with tears in her eyes.

Her brother squeezed her shoulder with a frown. 'I don't know. But I'll be behind you every step of the way, Squirt. Well, until your first spacewalk, obviously...'

Later, Carol overheard her parents talking.

'We can't stop her doing what she wants to do,' said her mum. 'We'll just drive her away if we do that.'

'But you know it's too dangerous, Marie,' said her dad. 'I just want to keep her safe. Don't you?'

'Of course I do,' said her mum. 'But she

has to live her own life.'

'Well, I'm not going to help her. She won't get a penny for college from me.'

Carol tried to talk to her mum about why her dad was so against her chosen path. 'Most parents would encourage their kids,' she said, feeling upset. 'Why doesn't he?'

Her mum hugged her. 'I can't explain it,' she said. 'You just have to trust your father.'

'Well, I don't,' Carol said, pushing her mum away. 'I'll do what I want, and I'll do it without his help if I have to.'

After that, Carol saved as much money as she could. She took after-school and weekend jobs that would fit around her fitness and study schedules. She became even more determined than ever to reach her goal, to prove that she could do this, and on her own if necessary.

But no matter how hard she worked, Carol was never going to save enough money to pay for the colleges she wanted to get into, let alone pay for private flight training.

The air force academy became her back-up plan – if she couldn't afford college, but she could get into the academy, then the air force would pay for her degree and all the training she needed.

Carol made sure that her school test scores – which she knew were good enough for consideration – were submitted to the academy for assessment. She sat as many college entrance exams as she could without her parents knowing, and made sure those results were sent, too. Once she was six months away from her eighteenth birthday, she went to the nearest USAF recruitment office and filled in her application. Once that was done, all she could do was wait.

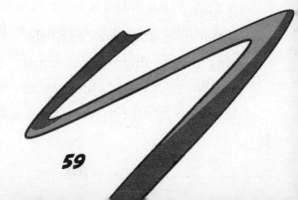

CHAPTER 8
A BIG CHANGE

The letter arrived on Carol's eighteenth birthday. She saw it buried amid the pile of cards from her friends that her mum had collected from the doormat. In one corner of the crisp, white envelope sat the USAF Academy crest.

They shared a look and her mum smiled a little sadly. Carol was suddenly terribly afraid. What if the letter was telling her that her grades hadn't been enough, that she hadn't been selected for the intake? What would she do then?

The money Carol had saved wasn't enough

for college. The air force academy was her only alternative. If she couldn't get in there either...

'Go on,' her mum said quietly. 'Open it.'

'Open what?' Carol's dad asked, looking up from his coffee.

Carol didn't answer. Instead she went up to her room, took a deep breath and then opened the envelope with shaking fingers.

It was a letter congratulating her for being accepted as a recruit at the United States Air Force Academy! She was listed in the next intake, which was due to begin the following week.

Carol sat down on her bed, feeling light-headed. She'd done it. She'd been accepted! This was the beginning of her career path, to space – as long as she got through basic training and on to the cadet programme. Carol could barely believe it.

She went back downstairs to find her parents both waiting in the kitchen. It was obvious that her mum had explained what the letter was.

'Well?' her dad asked.

Carol looked at her mum. 'I got in. They... they want me.'

Her mum smiled, but her dad stood up with a dark look on his face. 'You can't go. I won't allow it.'

'You can't stop me. It's not your decision, Dad.'

'Yeah? Well, you're living in my house. My house, my rules.'

'Wait, wait,' said Carol's mum, holding up her hands. 'Look, let's all just calm down. It's Carol's birthday, let's just celebrate that.'

Carol tried to enjoy the day, but all she could think about was what her dad had said. He was never going to support her, she knew that. If she didn't take this opportunity now, she might never get another. This was her chance – probably her only one.

That night, Carol hugged her mum before going to bed. Then she packed a bag with clothes and a photograph of her family from back when she and her brothers were little kids. She packed another bag with as many study books as she could carry and slipped the letter from the academy inside.

Then Carol climbed out of her bedroom window and shimmied down the tree outside. When she got to the ground, she looked back at her family home.

'Bye,' she whispered. 'I hope I can come back someday. But I have to do this. I have to.'

Carol sent a message to her brothers, telling them that she was fine and could they please check on their mum to make sure she was okay. Next she went to the bus station and bought a ticket to Colorado Springs, which was the closest city to the academy's campus. It would take two days to get there by road, but she had to save as much money as she could and flying would be too expensive.

The bus left in the middle of the night. Carol watched the lights of her hometown disappear behind her with a book open on her knees. It was going to be a long trip, and she had to make sure it was worth it.

* * *

On Carol's first day of basic cadet training, she arrived at the USAF Academy to find a group of fellow recruits all waiting together. Some were older than Carol and some were about the same age, but not one of them was younger.

'Hey,' said one girl, as Carol approached the group. 'I'm Casey. Good to meet you.'

'Carol,' she said, shaking her hand. 'Good to meet you too. This is going to be some day, huh?'

Casey laughed a little, obviously happy just to be there. 'It's going to be some life!'

As Carol grinned back, a door opened and an officer in the sharpest uniform she'd ever seen marched through it. He stood before the group with a straight back and square shoulders, and Carol thought about how it would feel to wear that uniform, to have those pips on her shoulders. Surely *that* would make her dad proud?

'All right, recruits, listen up,' he shouted. 'This is going to be the toughest week of your life so far, and it'll be followed by four more tough weeks after that, and then, if you make it through basic training, you will enter four further years of officer training for the United States Air Force.

'You'd better be prepared, people. This is the first day of the rest of your lives, and you're using it to enter the most prestigious military academy in the world. Do better than your best. Do your country proud. Do your families proud. Do yourself proud. Ten-*hut!'*

Cadet basic training was spread over five-and-a-half weeks, and the recruits' training officer hadn't been lying when he said it would be tough. Carol had worked physically hard to be there as well as studying as much as she could, but she still found herself pushed to every limit she had.

Some recruits didn't even make it beyond week three, dropping out and packing up their lockers while the rest of them prepared for another day of training. There were times when Carol thought she might give up herself – when she was staring at a calculus problem so complicated it took everything she had just to understand the question, or when she was carrying a heavy pack across rough terrain for yet another kilometre, or crawling through cold mud beneath a camo net at 5 a.m. But one look at the stars above her at night or a shout of encouragement from the rest of the class always got her moving again.

Higher, further, faster, more, she told herself, in those moments. *Just keep going. You won't give up. You can't.*

Carol never gave up.

CHAPTER 9
MEETING A HERO

Six weeks later, after working harder than she ever had before, Carol and the rest of the successful recruits went on to become fourth-class cadets at the United States Air Force Academy.

Carol was happy – her hard work had paid off, and now she didn't have to worry about not being able to afford college. Carol missed her family back home. She wrote letters to her mum and to her brothers, who all wrote back. She even wrote a note to her dad, but she didn't get a reply. She wished she understood what she'd done to make him so angry, but she was too busy to think about it for too long.

It was time to start her flight training.

Carol's first day in a cockpit was the most exciting of her life. Most of the other recruits had already had lessons in civilian planes, and she didn't dare let on to any of them that she had never even flown before.

It didn't occur to her to be scared as her flight instructor took her up in the two-seat fighter. There was no feeling that she might be sick as the aircraft picked up G-forces that pressed her back into her leather seat. The sensation of flying felt just as she had always expected it would – being in the air felt natural to her.

All the same, as Carol looked out at the slight curve of the Earth far below her, she felt as if there was something missing. She looked up and saw, far above her, Earth's atmosphere, and beyond that, the edge of space. She felt that pull, as she always did, to be out there, among the stars.

It confused her, this feeling. Where did it come from, this deep-rooted need to go into space? It was more than wanting to be an astronaut. Carol loved science, but it wasn't the quest for knowledge that drove her, or at least it wasn't only that. There was another feeling there, something she didn't understand.

After her first semester of training, Carol went home to see her family. She hadn't been back to Boston since she'd run away to join the academy, and she was nervous about what it would be like to see everyone again. Her mum hugged Carol for a long time, but her dad shut himself away.

'Don't think too badly of him,' Marie said. 'He's not well. He is proud of you, really, underneath it all. He just doesn't know how to show it. Most of all, he's afraid for his little girl.'

Carol wasn't sure she believed her mum.

'I know there's a reason he doesn't want me to be an astronaut, Mum,' she said. 'I overheard the two of you talking about it one day. Why won't you just tell me what it is?'

Her mum squeezed her hand and shook her head sadly. 'I can't, Carol,' she said. 'I made a promise. You have to respect that.'

After completing his army training, Stevie was deployed overseas, so Carol didn't see him again until she was already three years into her training and he came to visit her in Colorado. He looked so much older than the last time they had met. They hugged and Stevie ruffled her hair just like he had when they were both kids.

'Well, look at you,' her brother said with a grin. 'Not just little Squirt any more, eh?'

They talked about this and that, but in truth Carol didn't have much to say beyond news about her training. She worked so hard that she didn't really have time to do things off-base with friends. She felt she had to be the best at everything, the top of every class she took at the academy.

'You need to have some fun, too, Carol,'

her brother told her. 'It can't all just be work. I'm worried about you. Come on – I've got a surprise. There's someone I want you to meet. I called in a favour from a friend, who has a friend who knows this woman called Helen Cobb...'

Carol gaped at him. 'Helen Cobb? Not – not THE Helen Cobb? The ace pilot?'

Stevie laughed at the look on his sister's face. 'The very same. Want to go say hi? She's expecting us.'

Carol could hardly believe it. She was finally going to meet her hero!

'Aha,' Helen said, as they met, eyeing Carol with a look that was half friendly and half challenging. 'I still keep my ear to the ground, and I believe I've heard about you, kid. You're some kind of hot-shot flyer who's tearing through the ranks. Fancy breaking one of my records, do you?'

Carol grinned. 'One of them? Helen, I'm going to break *all* of them! I can, and I will. Just watch me.'

Helen threw back her head and laughed, then clapped Carol on the back. 'Now that's the kind of spark I like. You and I are going to get on, kid, I can tell.'

The three of them spent the rest of the evening talking and listening to Helen's stories. When it was time to go, Helen patted Carol's hand.

'Let me give you a bit of advice,' she said. 'It's not enough to be the best at everything. You've got to live, too. Because if you don't do that, you're going to lose that spark. And let me tell you – it's that spark that's going to push you ahead of everyone else. You hear me? If you make your life all about one thing, it won't be life any more, you will just be existing.'

Carol nodded. 'I get it,' she said. 'But getting to space is all I've ever wanted. If I don't get there, what does that say about me?'

Helen leant back. 'All I know is, it will mean you haven't broken my records!' She grinned. 'Keep in touch, kid. I see a lot of myself in you, and I like it.'

CHAPTER 10
AIRBORNE
AT LAST

A year later, after four years of training, Carol graduated from the air force academy as a fully fledged USAF pilot with the rank of captain. Carol was proud of herself and what she had achieved, but for all that, it was a sad day. Her brother Joe and her mum were at the ceremony, but Stevie wasn't there.

He'd been killed in action a few months previously, bravely defending the men around him when they were trapped by enemy fire. For months Carol was heartbroken. She missed her brother so much. Stevie had always encouraged her to follow her dream of flying, and now he'd never see her accomplish it. But thinking about him also drove Carol to work harder. Every time she felt as if her training was too hard and she couldn't continue, she would think of her brother grinning and giving her a thumbs up. At her graduation ceremony, she imagined him standing there with her mum and Joe, and thought about how happy he would have been to see her up there on the stage.

'My little sister, the fighter pilot,' her brother Joe said, as they stood together after the ceremony. 'Amazing, Squirt. Well done. Stevie would be proud of you.'

'He is proud of you,' her mum added softly. 'Wherever he is.'

Carol managed a smile. No one mentioned her dad, who hadn't come. Stevie's death had hit Joe Senior hard and he had taken it out on the people closest to him. Carol felt more distant from her dad than ever.

Still, despite her underlying sadness, Carol

felt as if she was finally becoming the person she'd been working towards her whole life. She couldn't wait to start racking up her flight hours. Carol was so keen to be in the air that she had applied to be a test pilot.

'That sounds pretty risky to me,' Joe told her. 'But then you always were a daredevil, weren't you? Remember those summers at the sound, when you'd throw yourself off the end of the jetty? None of us could ever out-jump you. Fearless, that's what you are. Always have been.'

'Just determined, that's all,' Carol told him.

She went to see Helen Cobb after graduating – they had stayed in touch, just as Helen had wanted. The two women spent a lot of time teasing each other about when and if Carol was going to break Helen's records.

'I'm proud of you, kid,' Helen said. 'Not just for graduating, but for your guts. You're going to go far.'

'Far and fast,' Carol repeated. 'That's a promise.'

When a letter responding to her application to join the test-pilot programme turned up in her pigeonhole, Carol stared at it for a full minute before picking it up.

Opening the envelope reminded her of that day almost five years previously when she'd found out she'd been accepted as a recruit. Carol was twenty-two now, and that seemed like a lifetime ago. She was an actual fighter pilot, fully qualified to fly combat missions, but she still had to stop her fingers shaking as she opened the envelope.

She need not have worried. After all, she had graduated at the top of her class. Of course the USAF wanted her as a test pilot!

From that day on, Carol distinguished herself as one of the best military pilots of her generation. She was so good that she was selected to fly the Stark-73 stealth surveillance jet that had been developed by Stark Industries. The aircraft was so cutting edge that she had to learn to fly it in a completely different way, but even that didn't worry Carol. She just wanted to keep flying.

It was while she was taking surveillance photographs of Afghanistan that her S-73 was shot down. In the crash, Carol suffered a broken leg and was captured by the enemy. It was a gruelling ordeal, but she refused to be broken – either by the crash itself, or by being a prisoner.

After three months in captivity Carol found a way to break out of her cell. She knew that being inside the enemy base could give her USAF superiors an advantage over the enemy, so she risked her life again to steal information about the base's position and capabilities. When she finally got out, she limped to a safe house, where she was debriefed by Air Force Special Operations Colonel, Michael Jonathan Rossi.

Rossi was so impressed by Carol's bravery and resilience that he persuaded her to retrain as a spy while she recuperated from the crash. Then, after a series of spy missions for the CIA, with Rossi as her partner, Carol began working with Nick Fury of S.H.I.E.L.D, spending time undercover to combat terrorist organisation Hydra.

It was an exciting life, full of intrigue and espionage, daring and danger. More than once, Carol's flying skills saved both herself and those she was working with. She didn't have super powers herself, but she was still a valuable member of Fury's team.

Later, Carol heard of an opportunity with NASA that reminded her of her childhood dreams of being an astronaut. Kennedy Space Center needed a new head of security, surrounding a new top-secret project. Carol wanted that job.

'I've got the experience,' she told Helen Cobb, on one of the rare occasions that the two women still had time to catch up.

'It's not actually going into space though, is it?' Helen pointed out. 'You'll be on the ground, watching other people go into space.'

'Who knows what opportunities it might lead to, though,' Carol said. 'Besides, there's something else going on down there, but no one will tell me what it is. Something big.'

'Like what?' Helen asked.

'I don't know,' Carol told her. 'But I'm going to call in every marker I'm owed. I want that job, Helen. Whatever they're cooking up in Florida, I want in.'

'Fair enough,' Helen said. 'Kid, I know you well enough to know that when you set your mind on something, you get it done.'

Helen was right, of course. NASA was pleased to have such a renowned and experienced member of personnel as the head of their security team, and with good reason.

The secret project Carol was in charge of protecting was a huge one indeed. Carol got an inkling of just how huge when she landed at Cape Canaveral Air Force Station, ready to take up her new post. She was met by General Bridges, who told her the core project that she would be overseeing at Kennedy was a joint one between NASA and the USAF.

'As far as the rest of the world knows, we're about to enter a new state-of-the-art research facility for new rocket engines,' said the General, as their military convoy swept into the Kennedy Center. 'But the truth is that we found something on the seabed just off an island in the South Pacific, and have been working for decades to raise it. Well, now we have, and the technology it houses will catapult Earth's technological development into the future.'

Carol frowned. 'Advanced technology, buried under the ocean? But how can that be?'

'Tony Stark believes it was left here millennia ago by a race of technologically advanced beings.'

Carol blinked. If Stark Industries was involved, that probably meant the technology was very special indeed. 'Advanced beings?' she repeated. 'Aliens, you mean?'

'Yes, captain, that's exactly what I mean.'

The fleet of cars drew to a halt. General Bridges opened his door and he and Carol got out. She followed him towards the biggest hangar she had ever seen – far too big for an aeroplane, or even for a rocket. They stepped inside and, for an instant, the floodlights inside blinded her. She let her eyes adjust, but even when they had, Carol had trouble making sense of what she was looking at.

Something huge and metallic was taking up most of the hangar. It was blue and silver, polished to a high shine. At first she thought it was a spacecraft, but then she saw something that made her mouth fall open.

'Is that a... a hand?' she asked. Then she saw a huge metal foot, too, and everything fell into place. 'It's a robot,' Carol breathed. 'Isn't it? It's a giant alien robot.'

'It is indeed,' agreed the General. 'And we want you to protect it, Captain Danvers.'

CHAPTER 11
AN UNDERGROUND BATTLE

Carol settled into her new role quickly. She spent most of her time around the hangar where the robot was located. It was a strange thing to see, like a huge person encased in metal. Carol found it hard to imagine that it had just been lying out there in the ocean. It made her wonder what other secrets were lurking out of sight, waiting to be discovered. She already knew from working with Nick Fury that the world was not as simple a place as many people thought. Most people on the planet didn't even know that aliens existed – and not only that, but they were right here

on Earth. Thanks to her work with Fury,
Carol knew better.

She spent a lot of time escorting the
scientists and engineers who examined the
machine as they moved around the base.
It was her job to make sure no one who
shouldn't be there got in to see the robot.
Carol made sure she was as informed as
possible about all aspects of the project and
read every report she could as it was written.

It seemed that the robot, when activated,
had the ability to fly, so the scientists and
engineers were hoping to find a way to
make that technology work for both NASA
spacecraft and air force planes. Carol kept an
eye on how this work was progressing and
made sure she understood the engines being
built as a result.

The main focus seemed to be creating
an aeroplane that could leave Earth's
atmosphere as easily as a jet taking off from a
runway. Well, if there was a chance of being
the one to test that plane, Carol wanted to

be at the front of the line. She spent every spare minute trying to keep her flight hours up. There was no way she was going to pass up any opportunity. She was a pilot working with NASA on their biggest leap forward in technology yet, and she'd already shown herself to be more than capable of flying cutting-edge aeroplanes. Surely Carol had a good chance of being chosen? After all, who would be better?

About a year into her assignment at the base, a new scientist arrived. His name was Doctor Walter Lawson, and something about him immediately set alarm bells ringing in Carol's mind. His paperwork checked out even when she did a secondary run, but still, something about this man worried her.

'I don't quite know what it is, sir,' she said, when she spoke to General Bridges on the day of Lawson's arrival. 'There is nothing solid to indicate there's anything wrong, but still... I've just got a feeling. Something's not right.'

'Well, he was specifically requested by NASA,' said the general. 'He's an expert in robotics, among other things. If they want him there, there's nothing you can do. But I trust your instincts, captain. Keep an eye on him.'

'Yes, sir.' Carol put the phone down and thought for a moment, resolving to make sure she knew where Lawson was at every moment – whether he was on or off base.

For the first week, Lawson did nothing but travel between the motel where he was staying and the base. When he was on base, he spent all his time in the hangar and hardly left, not even to eat at the canteen. In fact, he barely seemed to eat or rest at all.

Carol was beginning to think her instincts had been wrong when one night, long after work should have ceased for the day, she realised that Lawson was still on base. She'd been dealing with a delegation of air force generals who had come to inspect the project, and the debrief had taken her longer than expected. When she got out, she checked Lawson's whereabouts at the gate.

'He's not left yet, Captain Danvers,' said the guard, checking his log. 'He must still be in the lab.'

Carol hurried over to check, but there was no sign of Lawson. She ran back to the security hub and checked all the cameras until she saw him slipping into a small iron shed that housed nothing but the remains of an old well shaft they'd found when they originally constructed the base.

'Should I call for backup, captain?' asked the camera-room operator.

'No,' said Carol. 'I don't know what he's doing, but there's nothing of worth in that shed, just old junk. I'll check it out myself.'

When she got to the shed, there was no sign of Lawson. It was dark inside and there was no room for him to be hiding. She radioed the control room.

'Did he come out?'

'No, captain.'

Carol was confused. The only place Lawson could have gone was into the well shaft itself. But why?

She pushed back the heavy metal lid that had been fastened over the hole and clicked on her flashlight. Below her, the shaft vanished deep into the ground. On the inside of the wide metal tube were rungs forming a ladder. The light from her torch didn't reach to the bottom of the shaft, but she could hear faint noises coming from below.

Carol moved as quickly as she could down the well shaft.

As she got further down, the noises became louder – bangs and raised voices that sounded like a fight. A faint light swelled upwards, growing brighter the deeper she descended. There was something else, too – a faint vibration that buzzed through the well shaft and into her hands and feet, accompanied by an underlying sound in the air, as if she were surrounded by electricity.

When she reached the bottom of the

well shaft, Carol found herself in a huge cavern hewn out of the bedrock. A massive machine, the likes of which she'd never seen before, was lit up against the rock, pulsing with green-white energy.

There was a sound like a high-pitched whine building to a crescendo. The light was growing brighter by the second, as if the machine were powering up.

Walter Lawson was struggling with another man. The stranger was dressed in a strange sort of uniform that looked more like a military flight suit than regular clothing – it was white with blue flashes, and there was some sort of golden insignia on his chest.

Lawson looked different, too. Gone was the smart suit and white jacket he'd worn for the past week. It had been replaced by an outfit similar to the stranger's, but in black and red.

'You won't win, Yon-Rogg!' Lawson shouted. 'I will not let you destroy this world simply to feed your own power!'

'Traitor!' the stranger yelled back, as they fought. 'This planet is nothing but a forgotten Kree outpost. How dare you try to prevent me taking what rightfully belongs to our people?'

Carol drew her service weapon and aimed it at the two fighting men. 'Stop!' she shouted, over the noise. 'Stop this, right now!'

Neither of them took any notice. The machine behind them continued to vibrate, its light growing brighter and brighter.

'I won't let you do this!' cried Lawson.

'Walter Lawson!' Carol tried again. 'Stop this now, or I'll shoot. You're both under arrest!'

The stranger finally looked at Carol and laughed. 'Walter Lawson? No – this is Mar-Vell, of the Kree Empire. I am Yon-Rogg, also of the Kree Empire – and with the help of this machine, the Psyche-Magnitron, I will soon have the power of a thousand stars. Nothing shall stand before me – certainly not you.'

He lunged for the machine, but before Carol could fire, Mar-Vell had launched himself at Yon-Rogg. The two men fought but neither could get the better of the other. Carol tried to use her radio for backup, but there was no signal this far underground.

'Enough of this!' bellowed the stranger, Yon-Rogg. 'I don't have time for such games! You will be defeated, traitor!'

He pressed a button on the belt of his suit and the ground began to shake. Carol could barely keep her balance as chunks of rock began to fall from the ceiling. A huge, jagged ravine appeared in the rock overhead, as if the cave had been cracked open like an egg. The shaking grew worse. Then came the sound of giant footsteps crashing towards them.

Carol was thrown off her feet and landed on hard rock, the impact knocking the air from her lungs. She gasped for breath and looked up at the thing coming towards them.

It was the robot! Yon-Rogg had activated it

and the robot had smashed its way into the cave to reach its master.

'Now, Mar-Vell,' declared Yon-Rogg, 'you will die at the hands of my sentry!'

'Stop!' Carol got an angle on Yon-Rogg and fired a shot. It bounced off his suit as if it were no more than a child's rubber ball.

'Stay back!' Mar-Vell warned Carol.

'What is it?' she yelled over the noise. 'What is that machine? Tell me!'

Mar-Vell shouted back, trying to make himself heard over the infernal noise in the cavern. 'The Psyche-Magnitron allows its master to conjure up anything ever devised by Kree science. But I will stop it. I can—'

'Enough!' Yon-Rogg shouted. He lifted what looked like a laser gun and fired.

The blast hit Carol in the shoulder, a huge burst of searing energy that threw her backwards. She smashed down onto the rock floor, hitting her head hard enough to make her vision blur. Carol tried to get up again but couldn't move. She could only watch as

Mar-Vell battled the robot.

The metal monster began shooting fiery bursts from its eyes, the blasts pulverising everything they hit. Carol tried her radio again, but there was still nothing. The earthquake went on, the Psyche-Magnitron machine's whirring pulse reaching an eardrum-piercing crescendo.

Mar-Vell made one last-ditch attempt. He threw himself at the robot, hard enough to knock it off balance as it tried to fire at him again. It staggered and pitched sideways, its energy blast firing straight at the Psyche-Magnitron.

'NO!' screamed Yon-Rogg.

There was a deafening sound, a scream of energy as the Psyche-Magnitron exploded. The robot sentry was caught in the blast and was instantly pulverised into millions of tiny metal shards that flew in all directions. The shockwave shook the cavern, an earthquake that made the rock beneath where Carol lay trembling.

Mar-Vell launched himself into the air, lunging for Carol. He tried to shield her from the blast by covering her body with his, but she could feel the energy all around them, passing straight through his body and into hers.

I'm going to die, thought Carol. *And I never did get to space.*

She blacked out.

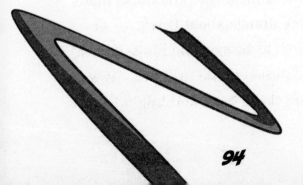

CHAPTER 12
A NEW SUPER HERO

Mar-Vell saved Earth, ridding it of Yon-Rogg
and his terrible robot sentry, but the base
was destroyed. Carol was in hospital for
weeks. When she was finally well enough to
be debriefed by General Bridges, Carol asked
to be discharged from the air force.

'You weren't to blame, Captain Danvers,'
Bridges said gravely. 'No one could have
seen what was coming. And you knew there
was something strange about Lawson – or
Captain Marvel, as he's calling himself now.'

'I was head of security,' Carol said. 'It was
my job to protect the base, and I didn't do

that. I... I don't feel that I fulfilled my duty, sir. I don't feel I have a right to remain in the United States Air Force, alongside men and women who do their duty every day, no matter what.'

Carol retired from the military with the rank of Colonel, but she was heartbroken. Her dream of going into space was over.

'What are you going to do?' her mum asked, when Carol told her what had happened. 'You can always come home, you know.'

'No,' she said. 'No, I can't come home. I'm going to move to New York. I've got a job as a writer and editor at a magazine. It's something completely different from my life in the military, and that's what I need right now.'

Carol found an apartment in the Village and moved into her first non-military home since she'd run away. It felt strange to be able to arrange things exactly how she wanted them.

She bought a television and the first person she saw when she turned it on was the Kree alien who had become Captain Marvel. The whole world was talking about him now – he'd become a super hero dedicated to saving Earth and all its people. Carol watched footage of him speeding through the air in his suit and wondered what it would be like to fly like that.

'Cold, that's what,' said Helen Cobb, when Carol called her to say hello. 'He must be absolutely freezing.'

'He's an alien,' Carol pointed out. She didn't tell her friend that ever since she'd been blasted by the Psyche-Magnitron, Carol had been having vivid dreams about flying, just like Captain Marvel – and it always felt amazing. What Carol wouldn't give to be able to do that for real. 'I don't think he feels things the same as we do.'

'I guess not. So, when do you start your job at – what's it called? *Woman* magazine?'

'Tomorrow,' Carol said, flipping through TV channels. Captain Marvel was on every one. 'Bright and early, I'll be walking through

97

those doors. Actually, I was going to talk to you about that. The editor has said I should put my own editorial team together. I've been thinking, do you know what Tracey Burke is doing these days?'

Helen sounded surprised. 'Tracey? She must be retired by now. Why?'

Carol smiled. 'She's how I first heard about you. That book she wrote about you, all those years ago — my mum got it out of the library for me when I was small. It was such an influence on me. It's what made me want to fly in the first place. Someone who can write that well — *that's* who I want on my team.'

'I think I still have a number for her somewhere,' Helen said. 'I'll find it for you. Beats me why you're taking this magazine job on anyway, though. Why not go into commercial flying? You could be an airline pilot.'

Carol flicked off the TV. 'No,' she told her friend. 'I've got to leave all that behind. Start over, do something completely new.'

'Fair enough,' said Helen. 'Still, you know what that means, don't you? Now you're never going to beat my records, kid!'

Carol couldn't help but smile at that.

Work at the magazine was a world away from being a military officer, but Carol threw herself into it, the way she did with everything. She liked interviewing people, and she also liked working in the office with other people – especially Tracey Burke and the enthusiastic young photographer Carol had hired, Frank Gianelli. It took some persuading to get Tracey to come out of retirement, but the first time Carol met her she explained what an influence Tracey's book about Helen Cobb had been on her, and Tracey loved that.

'It's always good to know you've made a difference to someone's life,' she said, with a smile. 'However small.'

'So come back to work,' Carol told her. 'Do it again! You've still got it in you. Talent like that doesn't vanish.'

'All right, all right,' Tracey laughed. 'You've convinced me. Let's do good work. Let's change some lives.'

'I'll probably end up leaving that to you,' Carol said, a little sadly. 'I feel as if I'm never going to do anything good again.'

Tracey squeezed her arm. 'Don't say that,' she said. 'You're just finding your feet, is all. I always find that when I'm struggling to know what to do, I just have to think about what would help someone else. It doesn't sound as if just writing words would be much help to anyone, does it? But I like to think I'm helping people tell their stories in ways they aren't able to themselves. And maybe I can help someone, like you, to work out what their own story should be. You can find your own talent too.'

The two women became close friends and Tracey introduced Carol to a lot of new people. It took a while, but Carol began to feel as if she was settling in.

She still kept having the dreams of flying, though, and they seemed to get more vivid every night. Sometimes Carol would wake up with her bedroom window wide open and the sirens of New York wailing outside. There would be a dream in her mind – almost as clear as a memory – of her stepping from the window ledge straight into the air and flying away into the sky.

Then a new super hero began to show up in news stories. It was a woman – she'd appear from nowhere when someone needed help, then disappear again, zooming into the sky just like Captain Marvel. No one knew who she was, and soon someone nicknamed her Ms Marvel. The name stuck.

Carol watched the shaky camera footage of the newcomer with a strange feeling – as if she should know who this person was but couldn't quite remember.

'You should do a piece on this Ms Marvel person,' her boss said one day. 'We could get the scoop on who she is, be the first place to reveal her true identity to the world. Work on it with Tracey and Frank – if anyone can get a clear snap of her, it'll be Gianelli.'

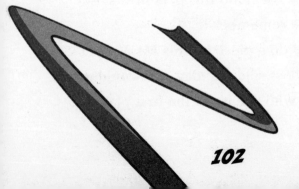

CHAPTER 13
FLYING HIGH

'There's something really weird about this, isn't there?' Frank said, a couple of weeks later. 'I mean, when this Ms Marvel has done her thing, she just completely disappears.'

'It's true,' Tracey agreed. 'This is New York City! You can't hide anything here. How can no one know who she is?'

Carol shrugged. The three of them were perched on a rooftop, Frank with his camera ready. They'd been staking out Manhattan ever since they'd been given the assignment to find out who Ms Marvel was, but so far, they'd not had any luck.

'Maybe she just wants to stay completely incognito,' Carol suggested. 'Maybe she's got friends or family she's trying to protect.'

They were there for hours. Carol eventually felt herself falling asleep. Almost as soon as she did, one of her dreams began again. Except that it didn't feel like a dream at all. She was on a rooftop in the dark, with the stars above and the lights and sounds of New York blaring below. She could hear someone screaming somewhere a few streets away, and all Carol knew was that she could help. She ran to the edge of the building, ready to leap into the air and fly, when—

'Carol!'

Someone grabbed her arm. Carol turned to find Tracey and Frank staring at her in shock.

'Carol,' Tracey said, looking her up and down. 'You're Ms Marvel!'

Carol looked down at herself and realised she was dressed in a flight suit a little like the one Mar-Vell had been wearing the night that Yon-Rogg activated the Psyche-Magnitron machine. It was even the same colour.

'Am I... am I dreaming?' Carol asked, stunned.

Frank laughed. 'Only if I am too! No – this is real! Can you fly?'

Carol looked at the edge of the building. 'I think so. I feel like... I feel like I'd be able to...'

'No.' Tracey grabbed her arm before Carol could step off and prove it. 'Just... try it here, first. Take off from the roof, don't jump straight off the edge!'

Carol did as Tracey suggested, leaping into the air. She didn't come back to earth. She hovered there, feeling an amazing power coursing through her body.

'My dreams,' she said, stunned, as she set foot back on the roof. 'They weren't dreams at all – it was all real!'

'This is amazing,' said Tracey. 'Is this – have you always been like this?'

Carol shook her head. 'No. It must have been the accident at the Cape base. When the Psyche-Magnitron exploded, Captain Marvel tried to shield me from the blast – I felt it pass through him and hit me. It must have transferred some of his powers to me!'

Frank laughed. 'Wow. You're a super hero, Carol! An honest-to-Betsy super hero!'

'I'm not,' Carol said, unable to believe what was happening. 'I'm just... I'm just me.'

Tracey put her hands on her hips. 'Well, sure, but the boy's right – you're still a super hero. Come on, let's put you through your paces! How high can you fly? How far can you go? How fast?'

'I – I don't know.'

Tracey grinned. 'Let's find out.'

Together, they began to test Carol's powers, with Frank snapping pictures whenever he could. First Carol flew as fast as she could. She lifted off from that rooftop, pushing up through the cold air until she broke through the clouds and out into the clear night beyond. She paused, hanging there, looking around her with wonder, and then she began to fly, the wind buffeting her face the way it had when she'd jumped her bike over that ramp so many years before.

Carol turned and plunged beneath the clouds, the lights of New York City coming up towards her, as if she were a meteorite from outer space about to make landfall. She began to fly circuits of Manhattan, pushing herself faster and faster until everything around her was a blur. Carol whooped and laughed as the air currents shivered against her, trying to slow her down.

She did that three times, as fast as she could, and then slowed until she saw Tracey waving to her from the rooftop and flew towards her, only pausing to do a quick loop-the-loop above her friend before coming into land.

When she touched down, Carol was laughing.

'What?' Tracey asked her, bemused. 'What's so funny?'

'Nothing,' Carol said, still laughing. 'Except that I'm not even slightly cold. And you know what? I think I've just broken one of Helen's records. And I didn't even need a plane!'

Tracey and Frank started laughing, too.

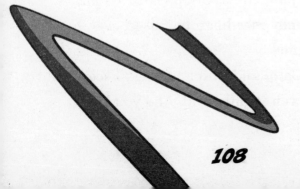

CHAPTER 14
HIGHER, FURTHER, FASTER

The next one of Carol's powers that they
tested was altitude.

'I want to know how high you can fly,'
Tracey said the following day, when Frank
had gone on an assignment elsewhere. 'Come
on, let's see!'

This time Carol didn't take off from the
rooftop. Instead she ran to the edge of the
building and jumped off, disappearing from
view. Tracey ran after her and looked over, a
horrified look on her face, but Carol bobbed
in mid-air, laughing.

'That's not funny!'

'Oh, come on!' Carol said, still laughing. 'You know I can fly! You've seen it!'

'Just because I know it doesn't mean I've fully taken it in yet,' Tracey retorted. 'It's not every day you discover that one of your friends can walk in the air!'

Carol grinned. 'Ready now?'

Tracey nodded. 'Let's see you do it.'

Carol shot away into the sky – but before she could even leave the skyscrapers of the city behind, she heard a commotion on the ground. It echoed up to her from between the buildings: the voice of a little girl, yelling, and older voices of men laughing.

She slowed to a stop and saw a kid of about ten standing in the middle of a short, dark alleyway, shouting at a gang of men who were standing around her with sticks.

Carol came in to land behind the girl and stood with her hands on her hips.

'What's going on here?' she asked.

'Hey,' said one of the gang. 'It's that new super hero chick. What's-er-name – Ms Marvel!'

'Get out of here,' snarled another. 'This is none of your business, sister.'

'I'm not your sister,' Carol said. 'And for the record, I don't really like being called a chick, either.'

'Oh yeah?' said another of the men, thumping a baseball bat into the palm of his hand as he stepped closer. 'And what are you going to do about it, *sweetheart?*'

'You really want to find out?' Carol asked, stepping between the kid and the men.

The guy smirked. 'Bring it on. I bet—'

Carol had floored him before he even had a chance to finish his sentence. He lay on the ground, winded from a punch to the stomach. He was the biggest guy they had, and she'd put him down in less than a second. She turned and looked at the others.

'So,' she said, nonchalantly. 'Who's next?'

The rest of the gang fled past her and out of the alley. Carol watched them go and then crouched down in front of the girl.

'Hey,' she said. 'Are you okay? What were

they doing?'

The girl wiped a hand across her face and then ran past Carol to a corner of the alley where there was a pile of old cardboard boxes. She pushed them aside and picked up a tiny puppy that cowered there. The puppy licked the girl's hand and whined.

'They were going to hurt him,' she said. 'I couldn't let them, but I was scared.'

Carol smiled, remembering the kitten she'd saved from the bullies when she was about the same age. 'That was really brave of you. Come on, let's get both of you home.'

By the time Carol made it back to the rooftop, Tracey was about ready to burst.

'Where have you been?' she said. 'I was going to call my friends down at the cop shop and see whether someone had turned in a lost super hero!'

Carol touched down with a smile. 'Just had something to do that was more important than breaking records, that's all.'

Tracey looked at her with a smile. 'I always

knew you really were a super hero. But look – there's only so much you can do. You'd better understand that straight away. You're just one person, Carol. An amazing person, it's true, but you can't do everything. All you can do is your best. Promise me you'll always remember that.'

Carol smiled. 'I will.'

Being an actual super hero was hard to get used to, but at least Carol knew where to turn for advice. Captain Marvel became a friend, which was just as well, as the name 'Ms Marvel' stuck even once Carol had gone public with her identity.

She became Ms Marvel to the whole world and became one of New York's biggest heroes. Carol worked with Spider-Man – and if anyone knew what it was like to juggle a job in publishing with being a super hero, it was Peter Parker! She worked beside Iron Man and the Avengers, too, helping to defend Earth against numerous alien forces. Later, Ms Marvel was invited to become a permanent member of the team. She changed her costume for the first time, taking on an entirely new look, aiming to make it hers.

Carol faced many foes and showed herself to be a strong and worthy possessor of the powers that had made her superhuman. She even managed to save Earth's sun from destruction when it was threatened by an intergalactic war, a feat that injured her so much she spent weeks recuperating in the Avengers' headquarters.

Somehow, though, Carol never quite felt comfortable as Ms Marvel. She hadn't been born with these powers like Mar-Vell, or gained them directly, like Hulk. It had been an accidental side-effect, like a shadow falling behind an object when the sun is at its brightest – something that would never exist without other forces to create it. Her strength, her ability to fly, her speed – Carol had never quite managed to shake the feeling that they weren't really hers.

Carol counted many super heroes as her

friends. But somehow, they didn't feel like her family. She never quite felt as if she fitted. She tried to fill the gap this left by helping as many people as she could, and she was loved for that. Or at least, Ms Marvel was loved for that.

Eventually, Carol was fired from *Woman* magazine because her duties as a super hero meant she was absent too often. Tracey Burke retired again at the same time, and when she became ill, she moved in with Carol.

Years later, when Captain Marvel died of cancer, Captain America persuaded Carol that she should give up being 'Ms Marvel' and become Captain Marvel instead, herself.

'I don't deserve the title,' she told him. 'I only got my powers by accident. If he hadn't tried to save me, I'd just have died. I wouldn't have become a super hero. They were his powers, and the name was his too.'

'That's rubbish, pure and simple,' Captain America told her. 'It's not where our skills come from that matters, it's what we do with them. You chose to do good, just like he did. Mar-Vell could have been as bad as the rest of the Kree, but he decided to become a defender of Earth instead.

'You chose to use your powers to help people, Carol. He wasn't born Captain Marvel – he chose to be. You can choose that, too. Who knows – maybe someone else will choose to be Ms Marvel now. Wouldn't that be great?'

Carol thought about it for a while. Then she decided that if she was going to be a captain again, she needed a captain's uniform.

The suit Carol chose honoured the original Captain Marvel – her friend, the one who had come before and the person who had shown her just what a good super hero could do. It had red shoulders and a blue body, joined together by a gold star that shone on her chest.

'Perfect,' Tracey said, when Carol put it on. 'Now you really are Captain Marvel.'

CHAPTER 15
JET POWER

Carol stayed friends with Helen Cobb,
even though, as Captain Marvel, she was
so busy that they rarely had time to hang
out. Sometimes Carol got the impression
that Helen was a bit jealous of her powers,
especially as her friend got older and was
no longer able to fly her beloved aeroplane.
But when Helen died, Carol was astonished
to discover that Helen had left her the T-6 in
her will.

The gleaming silver aeroplane that Carol had
first seen Helen fly at that air show in Maine
all those years ago now belonged to her!

'You've got to take it up,' Tracey told her, as the two women inspected the aircraft. Carol ran her hand along one polished silver wing.

'I will. It just... feels strange, really. The T-6 was Helen's pride and joy. It meant so much to her. I'm not sure how I feel about taking her seat.'

'She left it to you,' Tracey pointed out. 'She wanted you to fly it.'

Carol knew Tracey was right, and so she filed a flight plan, did her pre-flight checks and climbed into the cockpit. As the T-6 picked up speed along the runway, Carol almost felt as if Helen were there with her. Just as Carol was about to take off, she saw something dangling from the roof of the cockpit. She reached out and touched it – it was a piece of metal with a note stuck to it.

For Carol, with love from Helen, it said.

Something about the piece of metal niggled at Carol. It seemed vaguely familiar. She pushed the thought to the back of her mind. Unlike using her powers to fly, taking up an

118

aeroplane required proper concentration.

The sky was a brilliant blue as the T-6 soared into the air. Despite her abilities, there was still something thrilling to Carol about being inside such a magnificent machine. She thought of the records her friend had set and looked at the altimeter set into the cockpit's dash. What better way to honour her friend than by taking her aircraft back up to that altitude in homage?

She pulled the aeroplane's nose up and began to climb higher and higher, watching the altimeter's dial spin.

'*Come on,*' she thought, silently urging the machine on, '*You can do it. You can...*'

As the figure ticked ever closer to matching Helen's record, something began to happen. A glow in the air, bright as the sun, gathered around the aeroplane, glinting off its silver wings. The T-6 began to vibrate, juddering Carol in her seat as she fought for control. She didn't know what was happening, but she was afraid the aeroplane was about to break apart.

Carol tried to manoeuvre it back towards Earth, but still the T-6 kept climbing. There was a sudden, blinding flash, so bright that Carol had to shield her eyes, and then the sensation of spinning, as if the aircraft were tumbling through the air.

She tried to find the button for the ejector seat, but the G-forces were throwing her around too much. There was a huge boom, the brief feeling of utter weightlessness, and then—

—everything stopped.

There was no sound, no movement. There was only bright, white light outside the cockpit.

Then—

Boom!

Everything was back again, the T-6's engine sputtered as the aeroplane began to plunge back towards the ground, the altimeter spinning backwards, faster than Carol had ever seen it move. She grabbed the controls and wrestled with them as the ground grew ever closer.

It took all Carol's strength to get the T-6 under control. The plane soared over the airstrip as it levelled out. Carol circled once and came in to land, relieved that she'd managed to save Helen Cobb's pride and joy but wondering what had happened.

She jumped out of the plane and turned to look for Tracey, expecting to see her friend coming toward her, but instead there was a young woman jogging across the tarmac. As she got nearer, Carol realised with shock that she recognised her. It was Helen!

She was far younger, though, than Carol had ever known her. Confused, Carol looked around and realised that the airfield looked different, too. There were old-style cars parked everywhere, as well as more planes like the T-6. What was going on? What had happened up there?

'Well,' said the younger Helen, sticking out a hand when she was close enough. 'I guess you must be another new recruit.'

Carol frowned. 'Another recruit? To what?'

Helen tipped her head to one side. 'Aren't you here to take part in astronaut training? With flying skills like that I assumed you were joining the team of hopefuls.'

'Mercury 13!' Carol couldn't believe it. She must have come back in time to the point where Helen was herself training to be an astronaut! But how? And why? More importantly, how could she get back to her own time? Carol had to think quickly. After all, there must be some reason why this quirk in the timeline had brought her to this exact point, where she could meet Helen as a younger version of herself. 'That's exactly right! I'm here to join the team!'

Helen laughed. 'Come on, then. You need to meet the rest of the girls!'

Carol was quickly accepted as part of the training scheme, which had been assembled from skilled civilian pilots, all of whom were women. It had been Helen who had persuaded the NASA powers-that-be that the women could be an asset to the programme.

The problem was that to be considered for the astronaut programme, a pilot had to prove themselves capable of flying not just any old aircraft, but an air force jet. At the point that Carol had appeared in the timeline, women weren't allowed to join the USAF, so that meant that no woman would ever be allowed to train as an astronaut.

Helen had somehow changed that, though. She'd found a way to persuade the higher-ups at NASA that the women should be allowed to fly jets.

When Carol asked how, Helen just tapped her nose and grinned.

'Never you mind, hotshot. You just make sure you're good enough to make it worthwhile, you hear me?'

Carol didn't mention that she already knew how to fly a jet. She became part of the team, watching Helen fly her first solo flights, celebrating with this younger version

of her plucky friend. She hid her powers –
there wasn't any way to explain them. She
was just Carol Danvers, pilot and astronaut
hopeful. That was an easy role to play –
she'd played it for most of her life, after all.

All the time Captain Marvel was trying to
work out how she'd ended up in the past and
why. And, more importantly, how she could
get back to her own time.

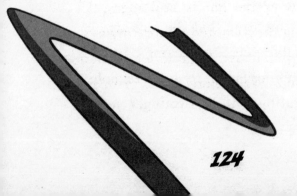

CHAPTER 16
A DARING HEIST

'Those rats!' Helen raged, pacing up and down the hangar.

'What is it?' Carol asked. 'What's happened?'

'They've dropped us,' Helen spat. 'All of us. All the women. They can't do this! We had a *deal!*'

'What do you mean?'

Helen threw up her hands, still angry. 'I had something they wanted. You're always asking how I persuaded them to let women train on the jets. Well, there it is. I bribed our way in.'

'How?' Carol asked, suddenly excited but trying to hide it.

'I gave them something. I don't even really know what it was, but I knew it was important. A fragment of metal that I found, years ago, in Peru – it was like nothing else I'd ever seen before. They wanted to run tests on it, because the composition looked as if it might have come from somewhere other than Earth.'

Carol felt a tingle down her spine. 'You mean they thought it could be... alien?'

Helen nodded. 'I told them they could have it, but only on the condition that they let women into the programme. It was the only way I'd let them have it, so of course they agreed. But now – now it turns out I gave it away for nothing.'

Carol's mind was racing. Alien metal, here on Earth, in this time period? Where could it have come from? And if NASA had had it all this time, what had they done with it? Could this have something to do with why Carol had found herself here in the first place? Could the answers help her find her way home?

'This is a joke,' Helen growled. 'I'm not standing for this. No one crosses Helen Cobb and gets away with it.'

She stalked from the room. Carol ran after her. 'Where are you going?'

'To get my property back,' Helen growled. 'If they're not going to honour the deal, then why should I?'

'Wait – Helen! Do you even know where this metal is?'

'It's inside a NASA lab,' Helen said, striding towards her car, 'I've seen them working on it.'

'But that means it'll be protected by NASA security! You can't just walk in there!'

Helen paused long enough to hold up her security pass with a grim look of determination. 'I can, and I will. Watch me.'

She leapt into her car, and Carol got in with her. After all, whatever had happened to the T-6 had dragged her back in time to Helen's past. Helen was clearly the key to whatever was happening to the timeline. Carol had no idea how she was going to set things right, but she knew she had to stick with her friend.

'This is crazy,' Carol whispered, once they had shown their passes and been let inside the building.

'You don't have to come,' Helen said. 'I didn't ask you to, did I?'

Carol kept watch as Helen jimmied the lock on the laboratory door. Together they slipped inside. Carol kept a lookout while Helen searched.

'Here it is!' she said triumphantly, holding up a sharp-edged piece of metal that looked slightly bent around the edges, as if it had once been part of something larger.

'Wait – I feel as if I've seen that before,' Carol said. 'Or something very like it, anyway. Where did you—'

'Hey!' The shout echoed in the corridor

outside. Carol whipped her head around
to see a uniformed security guard charging
towards them. 'You shouldn't be here. Stop!'

'Run!' Helen shouted, and took off in the
opposite direction, as a siren started up
overhead.

Carol followed her. They tried to get to
the exit, but more guards joined the chase,
cutting off their escape route. The two
women found themselves backed up against
a window with guards coming at them
from all sides. Carol looked out to see more
security trucks arriving, answering the call
of the alarm that was still wailing loudly
over their heads.

They were surrounded.

Then Carol saw something else – a glint
of silver in the sky overhead.

It was Helen's T-6! It was flying itself,
glowing in the blinding light of the time
fracture.

'Just surrender,' said one of the guards.
'There's no way out now, just be sensible

and give yourselves up—'

Carol grabbed Helen's arm. 'Duck,' she ordered, then smashed her fist straight through the glass. Shards exploded everywhere as Helen covered her face.

'What are you... ?'

'Just trust me – and hold on to that bit of metal!' Carol shouted. A second later she had lifted Helen clear of the ground and was flying with her out of the window, out of reach of the guards.

The T-6 veered straight towards them. Carol looked down and saw the piece of alien metal straining in Helen's grasp. The aeroplane was being drawn towards the artefact!

'What's happening?' Helen shouted. 'Are we – are you *flying?* Is that my plane, flying itself?'

'It's not a plane!' Carol shouted. 'Not right now, anyway. It's a time machine! And now I know exactly where that piece of metal of yours belongs!'

She flew straight towards the T-6 with Helen and wrestled them both inside it. The piece of metal immediately slammed itself into the control panel, joining the piece that Carol had found inside the aeroplane when she'd first got into it.

The T-6 began to vibrate, the glow of light around it becoming brighter and brighter.

'What's happening?' Helen shouted.

'I've got to go back to my past,' Carol shouted back, 'which means you have to come into the future. It's the only way to fix the timeline!'

The T-6 vanished in an incandescent blur of white-hot light.

CHAPTER 17
TIMELINE TWIST

Boom!

The T-6 vanished, taking with it the bright light. Carol and Helen found themselves surrounded by darkness.

'What happened?' asked Helen. 'Where are we? Where's my plane?'

Carol heard sounds echoing through the darkness towards them and realised that she knew exactly where – and more importantly *when* – they were.

She got up and helped Helen to her feet. There was a faint light in the distance and Carol began to creep towards it. Helen followed. They hid behind a rock and looked into the larger cavern ahead of them.

In it were two men in strange flight suits, battling it out in front of a huge machine that was pulsing with a strange energy as it started up.

'I've been here before,' Carol whispered to Helen. 'This is the day I got my powers.'

'What?' Helen said. 'You mean – that thing made you able to fly? What is it?'

'It's a kind of alien wishing machine. Basically, it allows its master to conjure up anything ever devised by Kree science – or that's what Mar-Vell told me, anyway.'

'Then – your powers – that's what you wanted? That was in your head and the machine just... gave them to you?'

Carol frowned. 'No... no, that's not... It exploded. That man there – the one with his back to us – he tried to save me from the blast. He's an alien with amazing abilities. When I woke up, I realised I had them, too. When the machine exploded, the blast must have transferred some of his powers to me.'

She turned to look at Helen.

'That piece of alien metal you found. I told you I recognised it, didn't I? It came from the Psyche-Magnitron.'

'The what?'

'The machine!' Carol said. 'It's generating a huge amount of power. When it exploded, bits of it must have absorbed some of that power, like I did, and were so powerful that they went spinning out through space and time. You had a piece in your T-6, didn't you? That's what turned it into a time machine. That fragment has been pulling the aeroplane through space and time, searching for the place where it belongs.'

Helen stared out at the Psyche-Magnitron from their hiding place. Mar-Vell and Yon-Rogg were still at the height of battle as the whine of the machine grew ever louder, straining towards a crescendo that Carol remembered all too well. She could see herself in a crumpled heap in the background, struggling to get up despite the blow she'd suffered to her head.

This was where everything had started for her, Carol realised – this moment was where she had become a super hero.

'You mean – if I also get caught in the blast when that thing blows, I could also get powers like yours?' Helen asked, looking at her with bright eyes. 'I could fly, just like you did a minute ago? Do everything that you can do?'

Carol blinked. 'No, that's not – that's not what I meant at all.'

'Why not?' Helen demanded. 'That's what you just said – that you were caught in the blast and got all these super-powers. You weren't meant to have them – it was an accident. So I could have the same accident and get them too!'

'But that's not—'

'I want to fly,' Helen said, interrupting her. 'I want to go into space. With your powers I could do that, couldn't I? So why shouldn't I?'

'We can't just change the timeline, Helen,' Carol told her. 'That's why we've ended up here in the first place! We've got to set things straight, not change them even more! Otherwise we don't know what effect it'll have on the future. We can't alter the entire world just to suit ourselves.'

'I can,' Helen said stubbornly, as she went to leave their hiding place. Carol held her back and for a moment the two women struggled against each other. There came the sound of rock being cracked and crushed, and the ground began to shake. 'What's that?' Helen cried. 'What's happening?'

'It's the robot sentry,' Carol said, over the noise. 'Yon-Rogg has summoned it. We need to—'

There was a huge roar of sound and light as the Psyche-Magnitron exploded. Carol looked up and saw the T-6 flying overhead. Gone was the cavern and everything around it – Mar-Vell and Yon-Rogg, as well as Helen and Carol's younger self. There was only the

T-6 rushing through time, moving quickly away from her on an airstream that was carrying it into her future.

I've got to get back to the plane, Carol realised. *It's going to go back to its own time – to my time. If I can't reach it, I'll be stranded here, in my own past...*

She rose into the air, feeling the power coursing through her veins. Carol couldn't change what had happened in that cave. It had happened, and these powers were hers. She had to return to her rightful place in the timeline.

Carol struggled to catch up with the aeroplane – she was thrown this way and that by a current made of time as well as air. She managed to grip the door to the cockpit but was thrown clear again as the T-6 shuddered and shook.

Carol forced herself to fly faster, the wind making her eyes stream with tears, almost blinding her. She got a grip on the aircraft canopy and forced it open just long enough to throw herself inside. It felt as if the T-6 was going to shake itself apart, it was juddering with such violent force.

Boom!

For a moment Carol was left breathless. The T-6, though, had stopped shaking. Outside she could see calm blue sky as the aeroplane flew on.

There came the sound of a radio crackling.

'It's good to see you again, Danvers T-6,' said air traffic control from the airfield. 'We thought we'd lost you for good, there.'

'How long have I been gone?' Carol asked, still a little dazed as she took the controls.

'Four days,' came the reply. 'We'd about given up on you, that's for sure.'

Carol looked at the altimeter. She hadn't quite reached Helen's record-breaking height. Still, she decided to turn back. Helen deserved to keep that, at least.

'Copy that, flight,' Carol said, letting out a relieved breath. 'Request permission to return to base.'

As she landed the T-6, Carol saw that
Helen's piece of metal was still dangling
where she'd left it with her note. *To Carol,
with love from Helen*. Carol looked at the
words and thought hard.

What she'd said to Helen in that cavern
was true. Carol couldn't change time to suit
herself. However, she'd ended up with her
powers, they were hers now. And it was up
to her to use them wisely.

CHAPTER 18
AMAZING ADVENTURES

Carol did her best to both honour Mar-Vell's time as Captain Marvel and to make the name her own. She did both so well that her adopted hometown of New York – and indeed the world – loved her. She saved the city from destruction so many times that, when she became homeless, after a neighbour grew tired of the antics that came with having a super hero next door, she was given an extraordinary apartment in the Statue of Liberty's crown. Soon, though, she moved back to the Village, keen to have as normal a life as possible despite the fact that she was so famous.

Meanwhile, she hid Helen's remaining piece of the Psyche-Magnitron machine away, wanting to keep it safe. It was dangerous, yes – but it was a part of her history. What had happened at Cape Canaveral had helped to make Carol who she was now, and she didn't feel that she could just discard that.

Jessica Drew – also known as Spider-Woman – became one of Carol's closest friends. The two women bonded over a shared sense of humour and the fact that they were both super heroes. It was nice, Carol always thought, when you could save the world and then just kick back and shoot the breeze with someone who really understood the craziness of super-hero life.

Her new neighbours were Marina Renner and her daughter Katherine, better known as Kit – or, once Carol got to know her, Lieutenant Trouble. Kit was adamant that she wanted to be Captain Marvel when she grew up, and she put together a costume that looked quite a lot like Carol's. Carol didn't mind – she loved looking after Kit when her mother had to work, and what was wrong with a girl wanting to grow up to be a super hero? Maybe Kit wouldn't be able to fly the way Carol did, but she'd find some other way to be amazing.

Things were going well, right up until the moment that Carol began to forget things. She'd arrange to meet Spider-Woman for a coffee and just not turn up. She'd promise to take Kit to the park and then do something completely different instead. It was totally out of character for Carol, and eventually her friends persuaded her to go and see a doctor.

'Just get a check-up,' Tracey Burke advised.

The doctor who Carol saw gave her a brain scan and was astonished by what she found.

'The human brain has two cerebral hemispheres, made up of different lobes,' the doctor explained, pointing to the scan. 'But as you can see here, you've got an additional lobe that has grown between the two. I think it's what controls your super-powers. Well, there's something growing on that lobe, and that's what's causing your memory loss. I'm sorry, but if it keeps growing – you're going to keep forgetting things. Eventually, if it doesn't stop, you'll forget who you are.'

'Don't worry,' Kit said, confidently, when Carol told her friends the news. 'I'm going to write a book, just for you. I'll write down all the things you've done as Captain Marvel, and from now on I'm going to keep a diary for you every day, so that if you forget anything you can read it and remember.'

Carol smiled. 'That's a great idea, Kit, thank you.' She watched as Lieutenant Trouble ran off to start the project, and then looked at Marina and Jessica. 'I don't know what to do,' she said. 'The doctors say they are going to work on it – but what's growing in me is alien. They aren't going to know any more than I am.'

'You have to take it easy,' Tracey told her. 'Less super-hero stuff from now on. You know the doc said the memory loss gets worse every time you use your powers.'

'Yup,' said Spider-Woman, crossing her arms. 'It's about time you learned to put your feet up for a change.'

'How am I going to do that?' Carol said. 'I can't just not help if someone needs me!'

'Well, as far as I can see you're not the only super hero around here,' Spider-Woman pointed out. 'I think the rest of us can take up some of the slack while the doctors figure out how to fix you.'

'If they can,' Carol muttered.

'Don't be a pessimist,' Tracey told her. 'Buck up. We'll beat this – but Jessica's right. Leave the big stuff to someone else for a change. Just for a while.'

Carol tried to do as they suggested, but it was impossible. She'd hear a cry for help and go rushing off without even thinking about it – and every time she did, more of her memories would vanish.

Then someone started to deliberately target Captain Marvel and her closest friends.

Strange things began to happen – enemies she'd fought years ago when she was still Ms Marvel would appear, goading her to fight them in a way that she just couldn't ignore. It was as if someone out there knew about the lesion and was doing everything they could to make it worse.

Things reached a head when Captain Marvel ended up battling a group of ex-wrestlers-turned-super villains who called themselves the Grapplers.

'I don't understand where they came from,' Captain Marvel shouted to Spider-Woman, as they tried to defeat the faintly ridiculous Battle Axe and her partner in crime, Pound Cakes. 'I stopped these guys years ago! I thought they'd given up their lives of crime!'

'You're just too popular for your own good!' Spider-Woman shouted back.

The Grapplers were no match for the combined might of Captain Marvel and Spider-Woman. They soon accepted defeat.

'Why are you here?' Captain Marvel asked the puffed-out villains, as she tied them up. 'What made you decide to attack today?'

Battle Axe shrugged. 'Seemed like a good idea at the time.'

Spider-Woman snorted a laugh. 'Well, have fun in lock-up.' She looked over at Captain Marvel. 'Come on, let's go. That's more than enough hard work for one day.'

As they were passing Central Park, though, they heard people screaming and running, clearly terrified by something behind them.

'We can't just ignore it,' said Captain Marvel, as she began to run. 'We've got to see what's going on!'

Whatever they were expecting to see, it wasn't two huge T-Rexs battling each other in the duck pond.

CHAPTER 19
OLD FOES, NEW DANGERS

'What is going on?' Spider-Woman cried, as she and Captain Marvel stared at the fighting creatures. 'Have I fallen into a parallel universe or something?'

'Come on!' Captain Marvel shouted, launching into the air. 'We've got to stop them before they kill someone!'

The prehistoric monsters were crashing around, destroying Central Park with their huge tails as they tried to tear each other apart. Captain Marvel tried to grab one so that she could haul them apart. It shook her off and turned with a roar to snap at her with its massive jaws – so she punched it right in the snout. The T-Rex collapsed, completely knocked out.

'Did you just punch a dinosaur?' Spider-Woman asked.

'A girl's gotta do what a girl's gotta do,' said Captain Marvel.

'Fair enough. One down...'

'... one to go,' Captain Marvel agreed, as they both squared up to the second T-Rex. 'Ready?'

'Oh yeah. Let's do this!'

Together they rushed at the thrashing monster. It came down with a massive splash, right in the centre of the duck pond. Several ducks quacked as they skittered out of the way of the collapsing dinosaur.

It was Captain Marvel who landed the blow to knock it out, straddling its neck and putting all her power into one final punch. Then she clambered down and waded through the water towards her friend, who was standing on the edge of the pond with her hands on her hips.

'Well,' said Spider-Woman, looking at the two unconscious creatures. 'Central Park Zoo is going to have to build a bigger fence, am I right?'

'I just don't understand it,' Carol said, as they walked back to her apartment block. 'What's happening? It's as if someone or something is deliberately sending stuff my way that they know I can't ignore just to make me use my powers.'

When they got back to Carol's apartment, though, there was more bad news waiting for them. The door had been forced open.

'This is weird,' said Jessica with a frown, once they had cautiously gone inside. 'It doesn't actually look as if you've been robbed.'

As Carol looked around, something strange caught her eye. There was a line of objects arranged on the coffee table that hadn't been there when she went out. She looked closer. There was a snow globe she'd bought from the Natural History Museum which had two T-Rex models fighting each other inside the glass. There was also a poster from one of the Grapplers' shows, as well as some of their toy models.

'That's super strange,' said Jessica. 'Did the thief leave them here?'

'They're mine,' Carol said. 'Various souvenirs I've collected. But I'd put them out of the way, with—' Her heart sank into her toes as she realised something. 'Oh no!'

Carol rushed to check. A panel had been ripped from the wall in her living room. A bag that had been hidden away inside lay discarded on the floor – empty. Carol dropped to her knees.

'What?' Jessica asked. 'What's missing?'

'It's Helen's fragment of the Psyche-Magnitron,' Carol said. 'It was a powerful Kree device that had the ability to conjure anything within Kree science into being. What I had was only a fragment, but it still had power and is incredibly dangerous. If it falls into the wrong hands... if someone tries to harness that power... I don't know what might happen.'

'Can you think of anyone who would have taken it?' Jessica asked. 'Who would have known about the Psyche-Magnitron? Who would want to do this?'

Carol stood up. 'I can only think of one person,' she said. 'Yon-Rogg! He was the Kree trying to activate the Psyche-Magnitron when it exploded. Mar-Vell – the first Captain Marvel – was trying to stop him.'

'But – wasn't he destroyed back then?' Jessica asked.

'I thought he was – everyone thought he was – but who else would know about this?' Carol said. 'He must have some plan that needs the power of the Magnitron.'

'But if he just wanted the bit of the machine, what were all the weird attackers about?'

'I don't know,' Carol said. 'But I've got to find out before he puts whatever plan he has into action.'

'Wait!' Jessica shouted, as Carol donned her Captain Marvel costume. 'You can't go up against him – it's going to make you forget even more!'

'It doesn't matter,' Carol said. 'All that matters is that I stop him. Whatever Yon-Rogg's planning – if he wins, the whole planet will suffer!'

She leapt out of the window and flew straight up. The renegade Kree wasn't the sort to hide, and she had a hunch he wanted her to know he was there. That's what all the games had been about, all the goading. Captain Marvel had defeated him once. Now Yon-Rogg wanted to prove that it couldn't happen again.

There, squatting heavily over New York was a huge and thunderous cloud, as if a thousand storms had converged right above the city. Hovering beneath it, his arms outstretched, was Yon-Rogg himself.

'Whatever it is you're doing,' Captain Marvel shouted, 'stop it, right now!'

The alien spun slowly to look at her, an evil grin spreading across his face. 'Aha. I've been expecting you. You can't stop this, Captain Marvel.'

She felt a sharp pain stab through her head. Yon-Rogg must have seen her wince, because he laughed.

'You can feel it, can't you? That little bit of me inside your mind?'

'What?' Captain Marvel asked, trying to focus around the pain.

'Haven't you figured it out yet? When the Psyche-Magnitron exploded, a part of me embedded itself into your brain. It's been growing there ever since. Now we're connected, and I can see everything inside you – all your memories, everything you ever wanted. I can make any of them appear, thanks to the power of the Psyche-Magnitron.'

Captain Marvel's head was throbbing. 'We're... connected?' she realised. 'My disappearing memories... is *that* what's causing it?'

'Oh yes,' Yon-Rogg crowed. 'And with the addition of your Kree brain power and the capabilities of the Psyche-Magnitron, I shall be able to conjure exactly what I want.'

He spun away and raised his hands again. The clouds roiled and billowed. Captain Marvel could barely focus for the pain, but in the midst of them, she saw something emerging. There was an immense city being built before her eyes, huge and mighty.

'Behold,' declared Yon-Rogg, 'the lost city of Kree-Lar! It will smash New York and take its place, and I shall be declared King over all! You stole everything from me, Carol Danvers, and now you will help me take it back – whether you like it or not.'

'*Hey, girl!*' The voice was coming from her earpiece – it was Spider-Woman!

Captain Marvel frowned, trying to concentrate on her friend's words despite the pain in her head.

'*Listen, I don't know what he's doing, but there's something happening all over the world.*'

People are reporting these huge robot things...
They must have been buried for who-knows
how long! They're smashing their way up to the
surface — and they're all flying your way!'

'My sentries,' declared Yon-Rogg, as
Carol saw a huge metal robot blasting
towards them. He looked at Captain Marvel
again. 'Your puny human brain does not
have enough power, but once the sentries
assemble, the part of you that is Kree will be
amplified to match mine. Then Kree-Lar will
live again!'

'Captain,' Spider-Woman said. *'How do we*
stop him?'

Captain Marvel stared at the alien, who
was once again laughing with glee. 'You
can't,' she said. 'But I can. Tell Kit she'll be
a great super hero one day. Whatever she
decides to do.'

'What?' Spider-Woman said. *'What do you*
mean? What are you going to—'

Captain Marvel flew straight up, away
from Yon-Rogg, away from the emerging city

of Kree-Lar, away from New York and all her friends. She flew as fast as she could, the throbbing pain in her head growing worse and worse.

If I can't remember anything, he can't use me, she thought, as she began to push through the stratosphere. And without me, he can't win.

She heard Yon-Rogg's ear-splitting scream of frustration as she shot out into the stars. Captain Marvel flew and flew, the pain growing worse and worse in her head, until—

—nothing.

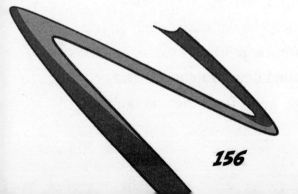

CHAPTER 20
HOME AGAIN

'She's awake! She's awake!'

'Kit, ssh...'

'But look, she's got her eyes open! Captain Marvel! Are you OK?'

Carol stared at the ceiling overhead. She didn't recognise it. Then again, she didn't know who the little girl sitting beside her on the bed was either, or the three women standing beside it, looking at her with anxious eyes.

'Carol,' one of them said, reaching out to take one of her hands. 'Do you remember me, girl?'

Carol shook her head and closed her eyes. Then something flashed at her from the darkness of her mind and she snapped her eyes open again.

'Y-Yon-Rogg,' she managed. 'Is he... ?'

'Gone,' said the woman who still held her hand. 'And so is Kree-Lar. Vanished when you... when you...'

Carol didn't hear any more. She'd gone back to sleep.

Captain Marvel couldn't remember anything in the wake of her battle with Yon-Rogg. For months afterwards, it was as if her mind had been wiped clean of who she was. Her friends were patient with her, trying to help her reconstruct her memories. Kit spent hours with Carol every day, showing her what she had written about the life of Captain Marvel in the book she had made when Carol first started losing her memories.

'It's all right,' Kit would say every time Carol couldn't remember something. 'That's what I'm here for. Tomorrow will be better.'

Eventually memories did begin to resurface, but they weren't of Carol as Captain Marvel. She kept thinking of a little girl running along a jetty and jumping from the end, soaring through the air as if she were flying before splashing down into very cold water. She could remember cliffs, and a bike, and a boat, and a man who always seemed to be angry with her, although she could never work out why.

'What about my dad?' she asked one day. 'I think I can remember him a little.'

It was Tracey who answered. 'You've never talked much about your family,' she said. 'I always got the impression thinking about your childhood was a little difficult, so I never asked too many questions.'

'I need to go home,' Carol decided. 'It might help me remember more of who I am.'

'You know that your dad died a long time ago, don't you?' Marina said, gently.

Carol nodded. It wasn't that she remembered, exactly, but she knew the information was there in the background somewhere, just waiting for her to find it again.

Her mother had moved to the Harpswell Sound summer house permanently not long after her dad had passed away, and so that's where Carol went. Flying into town brought back so many memories of summers long gone. She even bumped into her old friend Louis, although this time they didn't go for Brain Freezers.

'I'm back here to try to un-freeze my brain, not freeze it,' Carol pointed out, as he laughed.

Her mum hugged her, hard, and told Carol that everything was going to be all right. But Carol kept thinking about her father.

'What did I do?' she asked her mother. 'What was it about me that made him hate me?'

Marie Danvers sighed. 'He never hated you, Carol – he loved you, so much. I can't... I can't explain. He was afraid for you, that's all. He just didn't express it very well.'

'What was he afraid of, exactly?' Carol asked, but Marie just shook her head and wouldn't say anything more.

Then one day, hidden in the bottom of a wardrobe, Carol found a tin box. Inside were old photographs and a small sheaf of letters. When she picked up the letters, Carol saw something else beneath them – a strange-looking device, a bit like a remote control. She pressed the button on it, but nothing happened, so she put it down and looked at the letters instead.

They were in her dad's handwriting. Carol was reading them when her mum came in. She saw what Carol was doing and then the device that Carol had thought was some sort of remote. All the blood drained from her face as she bent to pick it up.

'Where did you find this?'

Carol scrambled to her feet. 'It was just in this box, with some of dad's things. I'm sorry, I was just—'

'This wasn't his. It was mine.'

'What is it?'

Marie Danvers didn't answer. 'How long has it been activated?' she whispered.

'It isn't—' Carol began, but then she realised that yes, the remote was making a sound. As she listened it gave off a low beep. She'd just been so engrossed in her dad's letters that she hadn't noticed.

'Mom, I'm sorry—'

Her mum didn't listen, going to the window and looking out at the sky instead.

'Mom, what's the matter?'

'You need to go, Carol,' said Marie Danvers. 'Go back to New York, now.'

'What? But—'

A noise echoed into the room. Carol recognised it as a sonic boom, like the sort a jet would cause as it broke the speed of sound.

'What was that?' she asked.

'Nothing for you to worry about,' her mum said, her voice sounding strange.

Carol went to the window. She could see a plume of smoke rising out of what looked like a crater that had been torn into one of the fields not far from their house. 'Is that a meteorite?'

Her mother pulled her away from the window. 'Carol – you have to go.'

'Mom, tell me! What's going on?'

From the distance came the sound of a car alarm going off. Then another started up, then another, each a little closer than the one before, as if a shock wave was moving towards their house.

Carol ran downstairs and out onto the deck, her mother close behind her. Something was coming towards them. No, not something, *someone*.

It was a huge woman with blue skin. Her arms and legs were as big as tree trunks and she looked as if she were ready to tear the world apart. She was heading straight for Carol.

An instant later, Carol was in her Captain

Marvel costume. 'Mom,' she said, 'Go inside. Or better yet, go get Uncle Richie to take you out in the boat. Get as far away from here as possible. I don't know what this is, but she's here for *me*.'

'No,' said her mother, from behind her. 'She's not.'

'Mom, please—' Carol turned and gasped.

Marie Danvers was dressed in a white-and-green flight suit with a crown-like helmet. It looked a lot like something Carol had seen before, only then, the alien Mar-Vell had been wearing it.

'Mom, what are you—'

'She's not here for you, Carol,' her mum told her. 'She's here for me.'

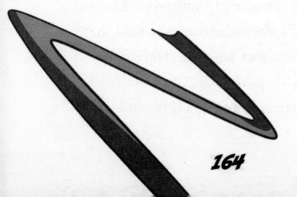

CHAPTER 21
THE TRUTH AT LAST

'Mom, what are you *doing?*' Carol asked, utterly shocked.

The blue woman reached the garden, stamping flat a flower bed that her mother had planted only the day before.

'TRAITOR TO THE KREE EMPIRE,' the blue woman bellowed. 'YOU WILL BE BROUGHT TO JUSTICE.'

Marie Danvers turned to her daughter. 'That thing is a Kree cleaner,' she said, her voice calm and clear, as if she were just reading out a shopping list. 'It's here for me.'

'But...' Carol spluttered. 'That's means

that you're – that *I'm*—'

'You are Car-Ell, daughter of Mari-Ell, Captain First of the Supreme Protectorate, Champion of the Kree Empire, Daughter of Hala by Bloodright and Starlight.'

Carol thought she might laugh. Either that or she was going to cry. 'Mom, stop it! This is crazy! You made pancakes for breakfast. You're just *Mom*—'

'Traitor!' bellowed the blue woman, again. 'Face me!'

'Yes,' Mari-Ell said to Carol. 'I am your mother.' She lifted into the air, flying just as easily as Carol herself did. 'But I am also a Kree warrior. Now go,' she said. 'Get to safety. This isn't your fight.'

Carol was so stunned she couldn't move. Then the blue monster lunged and Mari-Ell flew up to meet it. The two aliens met in mid-air. Carol's mother threw a mighty punch that knocked the Kree hunter back.

'Stay away from my daughter!' she cried.

The blue woman roared and fired a blast

straight for Carol. She leapt out of the way as the deck exploded into splinters.

Her mother roared with anger and charged straight at the Kree. The two figures struggled as Mari-Ell dragged the monster out over the bay. Carol was still trying to pick herself up as there came a huge boom and a burst of blinding yellow light.

'*Mom!*'

Carol shot out over the water, towards the light. Mari-Ell and the Kree assassin were locked in battle, struggling with each other.

'Get back!' Mari-Ell ordered her daughter.

'You can't do this on your own!'

'First I will eliminate you, Kree traitor!' yelled the assassin, 'and then I will crush your offspring spawn.'

'I'll never let you touch her!' yelled Mari-Ell. 'Never!'

'Mom—'

A blast strong enough to flatten a building punched straight into Mari-Ell. Carol was horrified as her mother was thrown backwards.

'MOM!'

She grabbed her mother to stop her from plunging into the ocean. Mari-Ell struggled in Carol's arms.

'Carol – go! You must—'

'No,' Carol said. 'I won't leave you. You can't defeat her on your own. We have to do this *together*. We have to combine powers.'

Mari-Ell grasped Carol's hands. 'All right,' she said. 'Together, then.'

The blue woman charged at them with a roar.

Carol focused all her energy on where her hand joined with her mother's. The power coursed through her, up through her core, the strongest she had ever felt.

The blast that exploded from their hands shot out like a white-hot laser. It smashed into the Kree assassin like a speeding train, throwing it backwards and out over the water in another huge explosion.

Something came flying towards them, straight out of the blast. The Kree soldier had thrown a spear straight at Mari-Ell.

'No!' cried Carol.

She caught her mother as she fell.

'MISSION COMPLETE,' the assassin declared. A moment later it had self-destructed, disintegrating into a cloud of molecules, as if it had never existed.

'Mom!'

Carol flew back to the house with her mother in her arms. She set her down on the ruined deck and knelt beside her.

'Mom... What can I do?'

Mari-Ell smiled gently. 'Nothing, my darling. This is the end of my path on Earth.'

'But there must be—'

'Ssh,' her mother soothed. 'Listen to me. I want to explain. I want to tell you everything. I want you to...' She coughed a little, '... understand.'

Carol nodded, tears in her eyes.

'I had always planned to tell you, somehow, in my own time,' Mari-Ell began. 'That time just never came. I was raised as a daughter of Hala – a warrior, first and foremost, trained for war from the moment I was born. For my first mission I was sent here, to Earth. I was supposed to monitor the planet and report back.

'Well, the first person I met was your father. He fished me out of the Sound when I splashed down.'

Marie Danvers looked out at the sun glinting on her garden and smiled, as if remembering that time, long ago.

'He was kind. He was a widower with two small boys to look after – a good man. For the first time in my life I wanted to do something more than fight. When I had to report back to the Kree, I told them your father was just a cover, and they believed me. But he quickly became more than that.'

'But – did he ever know?' Carol asked. 'About where you really came from? About what you could *do*?'

'At first I tried to hide it, as I had been taught in my training. But the truth has a way of coming out. Joe said he didn't care. We married, and the day that we did, I decided that I would never be Mari-Ell again. From that moment I was Mrs Danvers. I thought if I hid my true self away, that I could protect us all from the Kree.'

'Well, it kind of worked,' Carol pointed out. 'Until now, anyway.'

Mari-Ell smiled sadly. 'But hiding who you really are from those who love you causes its own problems. At first, when you came along, we were so happy. I remember your dad holding you in the hospital when I gave you your Kree name. Car-Ell. It means "Champion". And do you know what your dad said? He stroked your cheek and swore he'd keep you safe. "I'm going to protect her now, Marie. She's my daughter. I'm not going to let them touch her. I'm not going to let anything happen to her. That's on me."'

Carol tried to imagine her dad holding that tiny version of her. Then she remembered all those times he had been angry at her as she was growing up – every time she had crashed her bike or jumped off the jetty. Every time she had said she wanted to be an astronaut, every time she had talked about going into space.

It was because he knew, she thought. *He knew what was out there, waiting for me.*

'For all Joe's worrying,' her mother went on, 'I knew that I was the only one who could protect you from the Kree. But I was also the one who would bring them right to you. Because sooner or later, they would come looking for me. So I turned off my tracker – the device you found – and made Joe hide it away. I hid everything away, Car-Ell, do you understand? Everything that made me Kree. Everything that made me the person your dad had fallen in love with.

'I did it to keep you safe, but it meant I wasn't the whole person I had been before. And soon, neither was your father. He saw Kree threats everywhere. He was always afraid that something would happen to you, and he missed the real me. That was what made him angry, Carol. It made him angry, and then it made him mean.'

Carol stared up into the sky. 'That was why he wouldn't pay for me to go to college? Because he didn't want me to go to space. He didn't want me to find that part of myself – that part of *you*. And when the Psyche-Magnitron exploded... that wasn't what gave me my powers, was it?'

Her mother reached out and squeezed her hand with a faint smile. 'No. You already had them, Car-Ell. That accident just activated them. You've always been a daughter of Hala. Those powers have always been yours.'

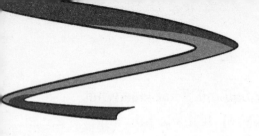

EPILOGUE:
TO THE
STARS

Captain Marvel blinked. Her breath came out as steam in the cold air as she remembered where she was – high above the Arctic circle, watching a huge metal robot tear its way out of the ice. But she knew what it was now – she'd come up against a Kree sentry like this before. There was no way this one was going to get the better of her now.

Robots, she thought. *It's always robots.*

Carol blasted down through the cold air, flying straight towards the massive machine. It must have been another one left on Earth long ago, just like that one she'd first seen back when she was assigned to security at the Kennedy Center.

The robot had almost smashed its way free of the glacier now and was standing, tall as a building, shaking the remaining shards of ice from its arms, only one leg still trapped in the ice. It was huge, its metal torso gleaming in the cold Arctic sun.

She crashed into its chest at full pelt with her arms outstretched. The impact reverberated up her arms, making her head ring, but Captain Marvel shook off the shock. The robot teetered but righted itself, one huge hand swatting her away. The super hero ducked and wove through the cold air, deftly avoiding the machine's grip.

The robot's free foot lit up, and Captain Marvel realised it was trying to take off. It had attempted to activate its rocket boosters, but there was obviously still ice inside its mechanisms because nothing happened. The machine looked down at itself, almost as if it was confused.

This time Captain Marvel aimed straight for its knee joints. If it activated its boosters it would be directing the power of a megatonne bomb blast straight down into the glacier! If she didn't stop it...

Captain Marvel slammed into the robot's legs. The free one shattered at the knee with a sound like two train carriages shearing together at speed. Sparks shot into the air as the lights went out on the severed leg.

The robot tried to smash her into the ground, but Captain Marvel slipped through its fingers again.

'*Captain Marvel?*' Spider-Woman's voice echoed over the microphone in her suit. '*Are you—*'

'Little busy right now,' Captain Marvel shouted. 'Call you back!'

The robot's severed leg was still sending out sparks as she doubled back and zoomed towards its other thigh. The machine was still trying to activate its remaining booster, but it saw her coming. This time she was a fraction of a second too late to dodge out of its way. One hand thumped into her like a bat hitting a ball and she went tumbling feet-over-head, out of control.

'Aaaahhhhhh!' Captain Marvel yelled as she spun away. She managed to stop herself from being thrown miles across the ice, pulling herself up and shaking her head to clear it. Then she plunged straight back towards the metal menace.

The sentry was trying to drag its remaining leg out of the ice. The crack in the glacier was spreading, the ice splitting open like the Grand Canyon. If it got its rocket booster working now...

Captain Marvel flew at it from behind and grabbed the giant robot beneath the arms. She dragged it up, pulling with all her strength.

The robot's leg came free with a sound like a huge cork coming out of a bottle. It immediately tried to power up its booster, shards of ice cracking from its frozen foot, but the booster didn't ignite. The robot twisted and turned, trying to reach the person on its back, but Captain Marvel wouldn't let go.

I've got to get it out of here, she realised. *I've got to destroy it completely, somewhere it won't do any more damage.*

She began to fly straight up, heading higher and higher as she dragged the sentry with her. It struggled and fought, but she wouldn't let go. Captain Marvel flew faster than she ever had before, shooting out of Earth's atmosphere and straight into space.

Space. Here she was, out here in all this nothing.

Carol still didn't stop. She flew across the solar system, heading straight for the sun, dragging the robot behind her.

When she was close enough, she spun herself around, gaining momentum before letting go at exactly the right second to pitch the sentry straight into the star. She watched as the alien robot flew into the sun's blazing corona. The robot flailed its arms and tried one more time to use its single rocket booster, but Captain Marvel had thrown it too fast.

There was a final, catastrophic explosion, so bright that Carol had to shield her eyes from the glare.

The sun's heat vaporised the Kree sentry completely. One minute it was there, the next –

Boom. Gone.

Captain Marvel hung there for a moment, among the stars, watching the sun burn in the darkness.

'You're still alive, right?' came a familiar voice, speaking into her ear again. *'I refuse to believe that robot dude was too much for you.'*

Captain Marvel grinned. 'Yeah, Jess, I'm still here.'

'Phew. Bad guy all gone?'

'Yup. All gone.'

'Great. Well, hurry back. It's taco night, I just decided. You could, like... pick some up

from Mexico City on your way home?'

Captain Marvel – Carol – turned and looked back at Earth, gleaming like a beautiful green-and-blue marble in the eternal night of space.

'I'll be with you soon. I just need a minute.'

She signed off with Spider-Woman and flew slowly back towards Earth. This was why she'd always wanted to get to space. This was why flying had always felt so natural to her, why it had always felt as if there was something out among the stars, calling to her. The powers she had hadn't come from someone else. They'd always been there, inside her, just waiting to wake up.

I am home, she thought to herself. Out here, among the stars – this is home.

I am who I'm supposed to be.

Carol Danvers.

Car-Ell.

Captain Marvel.

CHAPTER 1
SPIDER-MAN IN SPACE

Spider-Man had never been more scared in his life.

Under the Spider-Man mask, Peter Parker grimaced. He was hanging onto the side of a space rocket as it hurtled upwards. He was gripping on with all his might, but it felt like he was about to be pulled off the rocket at any moment and thrown back towards the ground. His Spider-Man costume felt cold against his skin.

As the rocket climbed higher and higher, he looked back down. This was a mistake. He had no way of telling exactly how far he was from the ground, but it was very, very high up.

'Hey, I can see home from here!' he said. It was true. As well as the skyscrapers of Manhattan, he could see all the way to the small suburb of Forest Hills in Queens, where he lived.

'How did you get yourself into this one, Spidey?' he asked himself.

It had all happened so quickly. Peter Parker had been on a high-school trip to see the launch of experimental space shuttle, *Osborn-6*. However, within seconds of the shuttle taking off, it was obvious that something was wrong. The shuttle was moving too slowly and alarms were sounding all around the viewing station.

Peter had raced away from the rest of his class to change into his Spider-Man costume. He was already wearing the full red-and-blue bodysuit, with a spider logo on the front, under his school clothes. Peter had quickly put on the Spider-Man gloves and boots that

were hidden in his backpack. The Spider-
Man mask had gone on last; this was the
part that made him feel like he had really
changed – like he had become someone
completely different.

As Spider-Man, he had rushed to the
Oscorp launch pad and talked to the
ground-control staff. Together they had
persuaded the pilot of a light jet plane to fly
him close enough to jump onto *Osborn-6*.

Now he was clinging on to the side of the
space shuttle for dear life.

'Spider-Man! Can you hear me?' crackled a
voice in his ear.

'Yes, of course I can!' said Spider-Man,
before he remembered who he was talking to.
He had been given an earpiece before he took
off, and he was talking to Mission Control.

'You need to find a way to separate the
rocket from the capsule with the astronauts,'
said the voice in his ear.

'Sure, that sounds fine,' said Spider-Man.
'Should be easy. I mean, it's not exactly

rocket science!'

Mission Control didn't reply.

Astronaut John Jameson III was aboard the shuttle, in a capsule connected to the rocket. John Jameson was the son of J. Jonah Jameson, the editor-in-chief of the *Daily Bugle* newspaper.

'Hey, could you do me a favour?' said Spider-Man to Mission Control. 'If there are any journalists from the *Daily Bugle* in the control room with you, could you ask them to write something nice about me? That would be cool!' He could do with some good press right now.

Spider-Man knew he shouldn't look down again. It was only going to make him more scared. The ground was too far away. He looked down again.

'Is this going to be more complicated than pulling out a bunch of wires?' he asked, trying to keep the fear out of his voice. 'Because otherwise all the movies I have seen have lied to me.'

'We're sure you can do this, Spider-Man,'
said Mission Control, but the voice at the
other end didn't sound too confident. 'Just
move upwards to the big panel above you.'

Spidey was slowly inching his way up the
rocket, trying not to think about how fast he
was going or how it was becoming harder to
breathe.

'I think I've found the right panel,' he told
Mission Control. 'Hey! There's a red wire
and a blue wire! I'm pulling the red one.'

BOOM!

The main capsule flew away from the
rocket, just like it was supposed to.
Spider-Man smiled under his mask as he held
onto the falling capsule. A feeling of relief
spread from the tip of his forehead, down
through the rest of his body. He had done it.
Spider-Man had saved the day!

Any moment now the parachute in the
capsule would open and they would all glide
gently to the Earth. Any moment now...

The parachute wasn't opening.

Now, instead of rising too quickly, he was falling too quickly. He was going to have to do something. Fast.

'Hello? Scientist guys in my ear? The parachute in the capsule isn't working! Any idea how I get it open again?' he asked, but there was no response. The earpiece had lost its connection to Mission Control.

For a second, he froze. What did he, a teenager from Queens, think he was doing, trying to save a space shuttle? And now it was all going wrong and it was entirely his fault!

What was he going to do?

Spider-Man spent a few seconds banging on the side of the capsule. He was trying to release the parachute, but also it made him feel better. If only he was a real spider, he thought to himself. Then he could just float away.

Wait a minute... maybe spiders were the answer! Some spiders used their threads to float through the wind on air currents. He remembered watching a documentary

about it with his Uncle Ben. It was called
'ballooning', and it happened when spiders
spun triangular parachutes to catch the wind.
Maybe he could do the same!

Working faster than he ever could have
thought possible, Spider-Man started to
create a large triangular net, using the
mechanical web-shooters in his wrists. As he
spun and spun, a makeshift parachute started
to take shape.

It was working! Although there were holes
in the net, it was slowing the descent of the
astronauts' capsule, and he could use it to
steer the capsule towards the East River,
which separated Manhattan and Queens.
The most important thing was to make sure
the capsule didn't crash anywhere where it
could hurt a lot of people.

The capsule was still falling at speed, and
Spider-Man was not at all confident that this
would work. But it had to. Everything was
moving towards him quickly and—

With a massive *FWOOOSH*, the capsule

landed in the river in a huge explosion of sound and water.

Spider-Man was thrown up in the air, then pulled under the water. He was spun around under the current so many times he didn't know which way was up. He kicked out, trying to push himself through the water. Then he surfaced, coughing and spluttering in the East River. He could see the capsule opening – the astronauts looked a little shaken, but they were safe.

Spider-Man looked up and saw a giant electronic screen advertising the *Daily Bugle* newspaper, with the words *SPIDER-MAN – MENACE!* staring down at him. J. Jonah Jameson had never liked Spider-Man. Even though Spidey had just saved his son, Jonah wasn't going to say anything nice about him. In fact, it looked like he hated Spider-Man even more now, for upstaging his son's big event.

Spider-Man sighed and started to swim to shore.